Follow Andrina Adamo's dancing career through these new editions of the Drina ballet books.

The Drina books:

Drina Dances
in Madeira

by
Jean Estoril

SIMON & SCHUSTER
YOUNG BOOKS

Cover artwork by Kevin Jones
Cover design by Terence Kingston
Illustrations by Jenny Sanders

Text copyright © Jean Estoril 1963

First published in Great Britain by Hodder & Stoughton Ltd
Second edition published in Great Britain by MacDonald & Co
(Publishers) Ltd

This edition published in 1992 by
Simon & Schuster Young Books
Campus 400
Maylands Avenue
Hemel Hempstead HP2 7EZ

Printed and bound at Cox & Wyman Ltd, Reading, Berkshire,
England

British Library Cataloguing in Publication Data available

ISBN: 0-7500-1267-6

Contents

BOOK ONE
A London Summer

1
Ilonka Tells the News

Drina was leaning on the bridge in St James's Park, gazing dreamily over the waters of the lake towards the familiar buildings of Whitehall. Behind her, and in every corner of the park, milled a cheerful Sunday crowd, for it was May and the hot sunlight bathed London in a dazzling glow.

But Drina was not really seeing the scene: her thoughts had gone back to Paris, the city she had left only the previous morning. She had gone to Paris for the very first time to dance Little Clara in the Dominick production of *Casse Noisette*, and that would have been wonderful enough. But there had been so very much more: Paris in the spring, with the chestnut trees in flower all along the Champs Elysées ... Montmartre so beautiful and quiet in the early mornings and the sleepy afternoons ... and then Grant Rossiter.

It still seemed a miracle that Grant Rossiter, whom she had been imagining in his native New York, had turned up so unexpectedly in Paris, and the time spent with him had been very happy, though at times overshadowed by the certainty that they might not meet again for years. For in New York, early the previous autumn, Drina had – then not quite fifteen –

fallen in love and the winter had been filled with an unhappiness and nostalgia that she had spoken of to no one.

It was not yet a week since that last evening at l'Opéra with Grant and afterwards they had said goodbye at Drina's hotel. It had been terrible to know that he would soon be more than three thousand miles away again, but now there was some hope of coming to terms with her feelings. Life, for her, had mostly to be dancing at the Dominick Ballet School, the first and most important thing for some time to come. Next year she would perhaps become a senior student at the Dominick.

Dancing, yes. But there was acting, too, for Drina had returned from Paris to learn that she was to act in the play, *Diary of a Dancer*, for a few weeks, while Giovanna Renti, who had not been well, had a rest. The original book had been written by Terza Lorencz, the elder sister of Drina's friend, Ilonka, and Terza had always wanted Drina to be in the play. Drina had refused in the first place because her dancing must come first, and also perhaps because it would be painful to act Ilonka in the play, the girl who had suffered so much during the escape from Lynzonia.

Now, anyway, the part was to be Drina's for a short time and in some ways it was a relief, for she had always felt a little guilty about her original refusal. And in the morning, instead of going back to ballet lessons and ordinary classes at the Dominick, she would go to a rehearsal at the Queen Elizabeth Theatre.

Life would be very full indeed, and perhaps it was just as well. Drina turned and began to walk under the soft spring green of the trees to the Mall, for she was to meet Ilonka and one of her other friends, Rose, in Piccadilly, by the gates of Green Park.

Crossing the Mall and continuing her walk through Green Park, Drina's thoughts were with Grant. Now, of course, he was back in New York and, as always, her mind turned back the clock five hours. It was nearly half-past two in London, so it would be half-past nine in New York. Nine-*thirty*, she added to herself, for Grant never said "half-past". If it was a fine morning, perhaps he was walking by the lake in Central Park …

Now, through a gap in the crowds, she could see Rose Conway standing by the gates. They had seen each other only the previous evening, for Rose had been in Paris, too, with the Company, but in a strange way it seemed longer than a few hours since Rose had stepped into a taxi at Victoria.

Rose was very pretty these days, for her two years at the Dominick Residential School in the Chilterns had improved her health and removed the anaemia and lack of energy of her early days at the Dominick. Unlike Drina, Rose was not well off. She lived in a small, over-crowded house at Earl's Court, and the boarding-school scholarship had meant a great deal to her. But now she was too old for Chalk Green and tomorrow would be returning to the Dominick School in Red Lion Square.

Rose waved and hurried towards her.

"Hullo, Drina! Isn't it a lovely day?"

"Beautiful! I'm so glad that summer seems to have come. How I hated the winter! It seemed endless. Did you find everything all right at home?"

"Oh, yes, fine."

"And did you tell them all about Paris?"

Rose grinned.

"Definitely! They listened with awe mixed with slight disapproval. Dad really is the end over 'foreigners'. But my presents were a great success. Where shall we go?"

"Back into St James's Park, shall we? But we've got to wait for Ilonka. I hope you don't mind? She phoned this morning and said there was quite a lot of news."

"Of course I don't mind," said Rose cheerfully. She liked Ilonka and was looking forward to making a threesome, now that she was returning to school in Red Lion Square.

They stood by the park entrance, and a few moments later saw Ilonka hurrying towards them, her dark curls bobbing around her face. Ilonka lived nearby in a flat above the restaurant called The Golden Zither run by her parents.

"I'm going to be in *Diary of a Dancer*," said Drina, as Ilonka waited on the opposite pavement for a lull in the traffic.

Rose stared.

"How do you mean? I thought you turned it down months ago?"

"I did, of course. But Giovanna needs a rest and Mr Dominick arranged it with Mr Campbell. I'm going to a rehearsal in the morning."

At that Rose looked absolutely horrified.

"But, Drina, you can't! You've got to be there to hold my hand. I'm scared stiff, going back to the Dominick after two whole years, and not even at the beginning of term, either. My only comfort has been the thought of you – I can't face that supercilious Queenie and all the others alone."

"Don't be an idiot! Of course you can. Anyway, Ilonka will hold your hand. And so, maybe, will Igor."

"I'm sure Igor's far too high and mighty at the Dominick to bother about me. In Paris it was different –"

"Rubbish! He *is* high and mighty but he likes you. I think he's rather taken with you."

"No, it's you he likes, but you weren't interested in him. He was jealous of your American –"

Ilonka arrived with a rush, a thin book under her arm.

"I'm sorry. I was delayed. Hullo, Rose! Drina, this is for you. It was published yesterday."

Drina took the book, which was the play of *Diary of a Dancer*.

"Wonderful! is Terza thrilled to see it in its new form? Just in time for me, too. Have you heard –?"

"Oh, yes. Terza told me that you are to take over the part. But you'll get an acting copy. This is not that –"

"Anyway, I'm glad to have it. I'll keep it beside the original *Diary*."

The three girls strolled into the park, making a very attractive group: Drina and Ilonka small and dark, and Rose much fairer and taller.

"Well, tell us all the news," Drina said eagerly. "How's the new term?"

"It is very well," said Ilonka. "Hard work, of course, but then that's usual. Queenie seems quite subdued just now."

"She has been ever since Christine left in disgrace. She's lost an ally," said Drina. "But if she's subdued, Rose will feel better."

"But not for long," said Ilonka darkly.

"How do you mean? Not for long?"

"Because Queenie now has another ally and soon she will be her old self. Her cousin Sylvia has come to the Dominick this term."

Rose and Drina stared and Drina said quickly:

"I didn't know she had a cousin. But then why should I? I'm not intimate with dear Queenie. What's the cousin like?"

"She reminds me of that English joke, the Colonel who has been in India." Ilonka puffed out her chest and intoned solemnly: "When I was in Poona –"

The others laughed and Ilonka went on:

"But it is not Poona. It is Paris, Milan, Rome, New York. She is far worse than Queenie with 'My mother was Beryl Bertram!' Always Sylvia talks about herself and the places where she has lived and danced; all of them, it seems, better than England."

"Oh, dear!" Drina groaned. "And she's been in New York?"

"Yes, she came from New York only recently, having been there for a year. While there, she learned ballet at one of the famous schools. She is a very good dancer, that one," said Ilonka, with gloom. "I do not like her at all, but she is very pretty. Her hair is redder than Queenie's and her eyes are more green. She plans to be most important."

"Well, Queenie won't like that, surely? She hates to be eclipsed."

"They are very – what do you call it? Thick," said Ilonka. "Always heads together. But there is other news. Drina, I've a special message for you. Hildegarde sends her love and says she is looking forward to seeing you. Rose, too, I expect, though she did not know I would be seeing Rose today."

Drina and Rose stood stock still in the middle of the path.

"Hildegarde?" repeated Drina. "Hildegarde Hermann? But she's in Germany! When she left Chalk Green because her mother was ill, she said she was going to stay in Germany and learn dancing there."

"But her mother is a little better and she so wished to return to England for a little while. I like her very much," said Ilonka gravely. "Never had I met her before, but she is a nice girl – so good-tempered."

"Oh, she's great," Rose agreed. "We were very fond

of Hildegarde. And she's at the Dominick?"

"Yes, for this one term. They agreed just to that. She lives no more in Freiburg in the Black Forest, but in a place called Dinkelsbühl. Later she is to live in Munich during the week and go to a ballet school there."

"But where does she live in London?" Drina asked, still astonished by the news.

"With some English friends of her father, in a flat in Sloane Street."

"So you'll be all right, Rose," said Drina, in some relief. "You won't need me in the morning if Hildegarde is there."

"It will take more than Hildegarde to make it easy to start again at the Dominick," Rose remarked, and indeed there were some grounds for her anxiety. Once, when Drina had been away from the Dominick for nearly a year, she herself had not found it at all easy to get back into the rhythm of things in London.

"But that is not all," Ilonka went on importantly. "You have other friends. There are twins, Sue and Joan Meredith … so much alike that it makes me dizzy. A few times I'd seen them, when the Chalk Green people came to London, but to have them every day is very strange."

Once more Rose and Drina stopped, and a thin man with five young children clustered round him said indulgently:

"Nar then! Nar then! Holding up the traffic!"

"But they left Chalk Green at the end of last term when I did," said Rose helplessly. "They were fifteen – too old to stay there. They were going home to Cheshire and hoping to go to ballet school in Liverpool. That is – they didn't *want* to. They were heartbroken –"

"Well, their hearts are mended, for they are at the Dominick. Living in Bloomsbury with some of the others whose homes are far away. They like it very much, they say. A nice lady looks after them. They love to be in London, though they miss the woods and hills."

"They adored the country," Rose agreed. "Goodness! What fun! You don't know what a difference all this makes. Now I shall almost look forward to tomorrow morning." A good deal of the tension had left her face.

"So all is well," said Ilonka happily, "and we can enjoy this lovely afternoon. You must tell me all about Paris – every single thing."

And, sitting on the grass by the lake in Saint James's Park, Drina and Rose did just that.

Two hours later, on her way home, Drina looked about her contentedly. Paris had been lovely … New York was, in many ways, the city where her heart was … but London was London, her home.

Suddenly Westminster Abbey was in front of her, its towers rising against the very blue sky. Big Ben struck five and she glanced up at the clock-face with affection. Dear old Big Ben, so much a part of her life.

It was summer. Old friends were at the Dominick and there was going to be all the excitement of acting in a play again. Life seemed very good.

2
Old Friends and a New Enemy

But the next morning, as Drina dressed in her grey and scarlet Dominick uniform, she was not feeling quite so cheerful. It was, after all, going to be an ordeal to step into an already successful play, and there was always the dread of what the critics might say. Drina had learned, since her very first appearance in the play *Argument in Paris*, to dread and fear the critics. Some, of course, were kind; others often seemed to have seen a totally different play. And she very much doubted if she would ever learn to take adverse criticism – especially criticism that sometimes seemed unfair – with equanimity. It was an inevitable part of the life she had chosen, but painful for all that. And even Catherine Colby, until recently prima ballerina of the Dominick Company, had once said that she had never learned to be indifferent to unkind critics.

Drina glanced into her little case to make sure that everything was there: her practice clothes, shoes, a towel, her beloved mascot, Hansl. Hansl went everywhere with her, a little black cat that had once been her own mother's mascot. For Drina's mother had been Elizabeth Ivory, a very great dancer, though the fact was not generally known, because Drina preferred to keep it a secret.

She wandered into the living-room, where her grandmother, Mrs Chester, was laying the breakfast table. Mrs Chester had brought Drina up since she was eighteen months old and was used to all the changes on her expressive face. Now she glanced at her granddaughter and asked sharply:

"What's the matter, Drina? Have you a headache?"

"No, Granny. I'm all right, thank you."

"You don't look it. I suppose it's this play worrying you? I really do think it was too bad of Mr Dominick to arrange it without consulting us. You deserve some peace now, and I'm sure you ought to get on with your work instead of running off to a theatre."

"I *shall* get on with it. I'll go to school as usual when the rehearsal is over and once I go into the play it will only mean the evenings. There's no matinée; only a five o'clock performance on Saturdays."

"It's too much for you, all the same. That play will take it out of you."

"I *have* to do it, Granny."

"Oh, you're so obstinate. You'll do what you think best. Well, get your breakfast."

Drina knew better than to say that she was not hungry. In the past they had had many tussles and she had somehow learned to eat when she did not feel hungry. She would have liked to gulp a cup of coffee and escape to a quiet square – Lincoln's Inn Fields, perhaps – until the rehearsal at half-past nine.

Her grandfather ate his own breakfast quickly and then left for work, with a parting:

"Good luck, Drina! You'll do it very well."

"I hope so," Drina said soberly, and was glad when it was time to leave. She caught a bus in Whitehall and, leaving it at the foot of Kingsway, walked up to the Queen Elizabeth Theatre. She paused to look at the pictures of the leading members of the cast. Carlotta Wertz, who was acting Terza Lorencz in the play, had a very sweet, rather sad face, Drina thought, and perhaps the sadness had been put there during Carlotta's escape from behind the Iron Curtain when she was eleven.

Giovanna Renti was pretty, too, with a delicate face and big dark eyes. Drina, who thought herself plain, sighed and wished she was as attractive as Giovanna. Giovanna was a good actress, also, and it would not be easy to match her performance. She was sixteen, surely almost seventeen now, but she had no difficulty in looking much younger on the stage.

"That won't be a difficulty with me, either," Drina said to herself, rather ruefully. For, though she was fifteen and a half, and often felt almost grown up, she still looked much younger. Because of Grant, if for no other reason, she had lately wished passionately that she did not look so young.

She had acted at the Queen Elizabeth Theatre before and the old doorman was a friend. Her short conversation with him made her feel much better and less of an outsider, and she walked along the gloomy passage feeling more confident. The theatre smell was all about her and she sniffed it with all her old pleasure.

She was early and the only person on the stage, under the harsh working light, was Carlotta, wearing black tights and a white sweater. She was down on all fours on the boards, playing with a black cat with white paws.

Drina stopped abruptly, feeling shy again.

"Hullo!"

Carlotta sat down on the stage with a bump and the black cat, purring, tried to scramble up on her knees.

"Ow! Stop it, Blackthorn! Your claws are too sharp! Go away and chase mice." She looked up at Drina, smiling. "You're Drina Adams? I'm Carlotta Wertz. How was Paris?"

"Lovely," said Drina. "But how did you know?"

"Oh, someone said you'd been dancing there with the Dominick. But goodness, how old are you? You look no more than eleven!" Apart from a very slight accent Carlotta spoke English very fluently.

Drina groaned and laughed and sat down beside her, disregarding the inevitable dust. The cat, seeing the chance of something more nearly approximating to a lap, approached in a friendly way.

"I'm fifteen and a half. Looking so young is my greatest cross."

"No doubt you'll be delighted when you're thirty."

"Other people have said that, but I can't even imagine being thirty. Can you?"

Carlotta, who was eighteen, frowned thoughtfully.

"With an effort, yes. It will happen; everyone tells me so. Blackthorn likes you – that's lucky. She's your cat Mitzi in the play."

"I know," said Drina, who was now cradling the purring black bundle. "She's beautiful. Is she yours?"

"Well, only half. She really belongs to some friends of mine, but she's living with me while the play runs. Blackthorn makes a wonderful actress. Cats are such chancy things; you can't train them as you can dogs. But only once has she misbehaved. She caught a mouse one night and dropped it at Giovanna's feet and Vanna yelled as though she'd been stabbed. She was very upset afterwards; it almost spoilt one of the most poignant moments."

"I don't mind mice," said Drina.

"You'd better change. Some of the others are here.

Wanda Werlingen, who plays Mrs Lorencz, and Basil Karl who plays the father. Your dressing-room is No 3."

Drina abandoned Blackthorn (alias Mitzi) and, taking her case, found her way to the dressing-room. She hastily changed her clothes, fastened back her hair, and put Hansl on the shabby, stained dressing-table. When she once more appeared in the wings, most of the cast had assembled and Calum Campbell, who was directing the play, was there. He was an old friend, for Drina had worked with him twice before, when she was in *Argument in Paris* and, later, when she played Margaret in *Dear Brutus*.

He greeted her cheerfully.

"There you are, Drina! I'm sorry to make you work so soon after Paris. I expect your grandmother wasn't too pleased."

"She *was* rather livid," Drina confessed.

"I was afraid so. But we need you. Giovanna's just about able to carry on for two or three more nights. You'll be on by Thursday."

"As soon as that?" asked Drina, rather dismayed.

"Yes, but it isn't a long part. You're only on in the first act and then again in the second scene in the last act. Have you had a chance to learn the part? Terza said she'd see that you got a copy to be going on with."

"I think I know it." Drina learned very quickly and, in any case, she had seen the play several times and already felt soaked in its atmosphere.

"Good! Well, come and be introduced and then let's get going."

The first act was set in the Lorenczs' flat in Lynzonia and the scenery for it was already in place for the evening's performance. At first Drina was very nervous, but after a few minutes the old magic took hold of her, though this time there was something very sad. For

Ilonka was her friend; they had been friends since that day at the Dominick when Ilonka was new and had cried so hopelessly because her father was still in Lynzonia and she might never see him again. Ilonka did not talk much about the last days in Lynzonia, but she had said enough to make it all almost unbearably vivid to Drina. Then, of course, Drina had read the *Diary* when it was first published and had been very upset by Ilonka's despair at having to leave the nervous little cat behind.

It was all too painfully easy to think herself into Ilonka's skin and, though there were interruptions while she was told her moves, by the time the act drew to an end Drina was deeply into the part. In the play Terza and her mother left for England leaving Ilonka and her father to follow a little later, and – alone for a while – Ilonka had to begin slowly to dance. Then she took up the cat and rested her face on its soft fur.

"Oh, Mitzi, I shall never see you again! I wish I could talk cat language so that you would understand."

And, saying those words into the dark and empty theatre, Drina felt an ache at her heart that was something much more than acting. Ilonka had another cat now, and her father was safe and happy in England, but probably they would never quite forget those terrible days, and somewhere in Lynzonia there might still be a cat called Mitzi.

That was the end of the act, but there was quite a long silence. Drina still stood with her face against the cat's fur, a little lost and forlorn, aware of the weight of Ilonka's sorrow and fear.

There was a murmur from the cast and Calum Campbell said:

"Yes. You've got it. That will be all right after another couple of rehearsals. Now we'll skip Act Two, at the frontier and in Vienna, and the first scene of Act Three, Terza's audition at the Dominick. Act Three, Scene Two. Terza's dressing-room. You aren't on at first."

Drina retreated to the O.P. corner with Blackthorn and watched the early part of the scene, the evening of Terza's first appearance with the Dominick *corps de ballet*. Then she was on stage again. Mrs Lorencz had gone to meet Ilonka at the airport and there was a mixture of rejoicing and sorrow. For they did not know if Mr Lorencz was safe and they feared he might never reach England. Terza went on stage and then a telegram arrived to say that he was safe after all. To the distant music of *Swan Lake* Ilonka began to dance; this time a dance of joy and hope for the future.

The cast rehearsed the first act again and by the time she returned to her dressing-room Drina was very tired. She had known all along that it would be upsetting to act in the play, and one thing was clear. She must on no account let her grandmother guess just what emotional demands it was likely to make on her.

Emerging in her Dominick uniform, clutching her little case, she was startled to find a tall and familiar figure waiting in the passage.

"Mr Dominick!" she cried, her usually pale face flushing red.

The Director of the Dominick School and Company grinned at her. He was regarded with much awe by everyone in the School, and to most of the younger students he was a distant, quite unapproachable figure. This was not entirely true of Drina, however, for circumstances had quickly brought her to his notice and she had often talked to him. But still he *was* the Director and she an unimportant junior student.

"I thought we might walk over together," said Igor Dominick, looking at her surprised face with some amusement. Then he added much more gravely:

"You were good. You'll be better than Giovanna. You *feel* it all so much."

"But were you there? I – I didn't see you."

"Back of the stalls," he said briefly. "I felt responsible. Thought I'd better see how you got on. But, look, my dear, don't take it *too* much to heart."

"I – but I can't help it. It's knowing Ilonka and – and all of them. Knowing she still can't easily speak of Mitzi or those days."

"Well, if you get too upset your grandmother will flay me. Mad, was she?"

"Wild, in a quiet way," said Drina, falling into step with him.

"She was always an obstinate woman. I don't believe she's resigned *yet* to your chosen career."

It was somehow startling to hear her grandmother called "an obstinate woman" in that tone. But then Igor Dominick had known Mrs Chester in the days when her daughter, Elizabeth Ivory, had danced with the Dominick Company. It was only the previous year that they had met again, with full knowledge on both sides about Drina's mother. Until the Edinburgh Festival, when Drina had first danced Little Clara with the Dominick, neither Mr Dominick nor Marianne Volonaise had known that small, dark Drina Adams was the daughter of the woman who had perhaps been the greatest dancer of all time.

"Granny says *I'm* obstinate," Drina said, as they left the theatre and turned towards Red Lion Square.

"So you are, and a good thing, too, or you'd never have been a dancer."

"I think she's resigned to me dancing now, but not to acting," said Drina, hurrying to keep up with his long strides. It felt absurd to be so small beside the tall, commanding figure.

"You may as well do both, since you've the opportunity." The Director of the Dominick looked along the street, a slight frown creasing his thick brows. "Altered, hasn't it, during the last year or two? All this new building."

"Yes," agreed Drina, looking at the latest office block, its many windows gleaming in the sunshine. "I like it in a way, though it's sad to see the old parts go. There's really only that one row of houses now, and the Dominick School and rehearsal rooms."

"Things must change, I suppose, but it isn't always welcome." Igor Dominick hesitated, looking down at her, and for a moment she thought he was going to say something of importance. But he seemed to change his mind.

They crossed the square and approached the Dominick, bright with a new coat of turquoise blue paint.

It was five-past twelve and classes were out. Students were streaming down the stairs as Drina entered with the Director, and she said nervously:

"I'll – I'll go and have lunch, then. Thank you, Mr Dominick."

But he stopped her, with a hand on her arm.

"Marianne and I, and probably young Igor, will be along to watch a performance one night. Good luck!" He went striding up the stairs, while everyone moved respectfully to one side, and Drina soon found herself surrounded by various members of her class. Rose was there, and Ilonka, also Queenie and a handsome red-haired girl with startlingly green eyes.

"Oh, Drina, how did you get on?" Rose asked.

"Really!" said Queenie spitefully. "The cheek of it! I wouldn't have believed it if I hadn't seen it with my own eyes. Coming in with Mr Dominick in that casual way. Clearly, going to Paris must have gone to Drina's head, like so many other things. I hate to think what Mr Dominick must think of her."

Drina always tried to ignore Queenie's unpleasantness, but she had a temper that was not entirely easy to control.

"If you must know, he watched the rehearsal and then waited to walk back with me."

"A *very* likely story!" said Queenie. They were words of which she was rather fond.

"Likely or not, it's the truth."

"Oh, we all know that you cadge notice from the great ones."

"Drina doesn't! You are always so jealous, Queenie," Ilonka cried, in hot defence of her friend.

"Jealous? Of dear little Drina?" But it was true; Queenie had always been bitterly jealous of Drina and Drina never failed to be upset by her dislike.

"Come on Sylvia," said Queenie loftily. "We have far more important things to talk about."

"So have we!" retorted Drina, seeing Hildegarde in the crowd. Her German friend looked just the same, her brown hair tied in a neat ponytail. "Oh, Hildegarde, I *am* so glad to see you!"

"I'm glad to see *you*, Drina!" cried Hildegarde, shaking hands warmly. During her years at Chalk Green she had learned to speak English fluently. "And Rose and Sue and Joan. Oh, I'm so happy to be back!"

"It must feel funny, though. You never really knew the Dominick."

"Only when we visited it from Chalk Green, but many people were familiar by sight. Oh, Drina, we live now in Dinkelsbühl: it's a wonderful place. You'd love it."

"I've never even heard of it," Drina confessed. "Is it

near Freiburg?"

"No, it's in Northern Bavaria, on what they call the Romantic Road. There are three lovely medieval towns, Nordlingen, Dinkelsbühl and Rothenburg. Dinkelsbühl's like a fairy tale, with walls and pepper-pot towers and beautiful gabled houses in all colours."

"You must tell me every single thing about it when we've time. You must come to tea just as soon as we can fix it."

'Thank you, yes. And perhaps you could come to visit us in Dinkelsbühl? We'll talk of it later. During the summer holidays, perhaps."

"Oh, I'd love to. I've never been to Germany." Drina adored travel and the thought of that distant city with its walls and towers immediately fascinated her.

"But you've been to many other places since we last met. Rose was telling me."

"If we don't hurry we'll get no lunch." And they pushed their way towards the canteen, presently getting near to identical twins Joan and Sue, who shrieked with excitement.

"Drina! What do you mean by going to Paris and then getting yourself another part in a play? Are you too important to speak to us now? You're quite famous, aren't you?"

"Don't be silly!" Drina said, almost sharply. "I'm not famous at all. Oh, I am glad to see the pair of you! Joan, is it?" And she grinned at the first twin, who smiled back and said:

"No, I'm Sue."

'Goodness! I'm not surprised that Ilonka is dizzy. It does take some getting used to. I did learn to take it for granted when I shared a bedroom with you both. I still wonder what will happen when the pair of you are in the Company."

"Our first solo roles are going to be the Blue Skaters in *Les Patineurs*," said Sue.

"Oh, it's all fixed, is it?" said Drina lightly, as they queued for the first course.

"Only in our own minds. Goodness knows what those in authority will do. We may never get into the Company at all."

"Oh, you are here, Drina!" said a rather lordly voice from near by, and there was Igor Dominick Junior, tall and dark and smiling across at Drina.

"Oh, hullo, Igor!" Drina said casually. She liked Igor well enough, in spite of his airs, but she had long since ceased to be impressed by him.

Lunch passed in laughter and chatter, and Drina found that she was very happy to be back at the Dominick amongst her friends. For two terms, after New York, she had not been as happy as usual, but now perhaps everything was going to be all right. For a brief moment her mind went to Grant – twelve-thirty in London, so seven-thirty in New York – but she pushed the thought sternly away. Thoughts of Grant had somehow to be kept for her few leisurely moments and before she went to sleep at night. She must *not* sink back into the terrible nostalgia that had haunted her all winter.

Afterwards they strolled in the square and then went upstairs to the big classroom at the front of the building. There were still a few minutes before the next class started and Sylvia Prenton – Queenie's cousin – stood at the window.

"London makes me laugh! It really does. Twenty storeys and they call it a skyscraper. Why in New York –"

This was what Drina herself had often thought, though not often said, but there was something about

Sylvia's tone that was decidedly irritating. If Sylvia had looked a different type of girl she might have delighted to talk about the city she had loved so much. Drina had often had to curb her tongue, fearing to bore people with references to New York.

She was a little startled by the feeling of jealousy that went through her as she looked at the red-haired girl. Sylvia had lived for a whole year in New York; she must often have walked down Fifth Avenue and seen the light change on those tapering glass and steel towers.

Sylvia was going on, in her clear, but rather affected voice that bore no trace of an American accent:

"It all makes me laugh. No one can know who hasn't lived in New York. The *elevators* here – creaking their way up two or three floors as though each creak will be their last! Why, in the Empire State Building you go up a hundred and two floors without a pause, just in a few seconds."

This was too much. Before Drina could stop herself she had said:

"You certainly don't. There are three elevators that take you to the top of the Empire State."

Sylvia swung round, her green eyes wide and unbearably supercilious.

"*You* would know, of course. Queenie told me you were too big for your boots. Why, I've *lived* in New York – in Brooklyn –"

"Oh, not in Manhattan?" Drina said sweetly. In Brooklyn Sylvia might have had a superb view of the downtown skyscrapers, but it was a strange relief that she had not actually lived in Manhattan. "Anyway, there definitely are three lifts. The first goes to about the eightieth floor, then the second to the Observation Platforms. The last takes you just a bit higher to the glassed-in part –"

She and Sylvia stood eyeing each other and Drina was conscious of the instant antagonism between them. It was an absurd argument, of course, and she had been silly to contradict the newcomer, but even without that she felt they would soon have come up against each other.

A moment later the English teacher entered the room and the lesson began. Drina settled down to work, but it was not easy. There was so much to occupy her mind.

The play ... Mr Dominick ... old friends back again ... a new enemy? She sighed and tried to give her whole attention to *Macbeth*. She had already lost too much time and must work hard. It would be terrible to get a bad report at the end of term.

3

Letters for Drina

After school Ilonka had to hurry away on an errand for her mother, and Rose and Drina strolled towards Piccadilly.

"It's so long since we were able to do this after school," said Drina, with a contented sigh, as, after crossing the top of Drury Lane and walking through a broad alley, they saw the Royal Opera House in front of them.

Rose stared at its impressive facade and a passing policeman grinned at her and asked:

"Hoping you'll sing in there one day, love?"

"No, dance. I'm a future ballerina, if you only knew it," Rose answered, with typical Cockney speed.

Then she added when he had gone:

"We must go to Covent Garden again soon, Drina."

"I know. It's ages since we've been. But I can't even go to the Saturday matinée while I'm in *Diary of a Dancer*. I wish we could go *this* Saturday," said Drina, as they crossed the road and studied the posters. "*Antigone, Le Baiser de la Fée* and *Pineapple Poll*. I just long to see *Antigone*; it's dreadful not to have seen it. But I don't like *Pineapple Poll*."

"It's very cheerful."

"Oh, yes, but I generally like the tragic or unusual ones best nowadays. And really modern music."

"There was a time when *Les Sylphides* was your favourite," remarked Rose, as they began to cut through the narrow streets of the Covent Garden area.

"So it was," Drina agreed dreamily. "I thought it beautiful. It was the first ballet I was ever aware of, before I really knew *anything*. I'm sure I've seen it more than any other ballet, too, but somehow it's spoilt now. I do love the music, but I get tired of the soulful expressions on the faces of the *corps de ballet*. I can't help thinking that they're probably in a draught, poor things, when they're drooping there in such graceful attitudes, and how awful it would be if one sneezed or began to hiccough."

Rose giggled.

"That's the penalty of being in the know. Didn't Bettina once say that when she had a bad bilious attack she was terrified of being sick right there on the stage? A sick sylphide really would be the end!"

"It would be simply terrible," said Drina, horrified by the macabre picture.

"Anyway, I suppose the day will come – if we make the grade – when we'll be thrilled to be sylphides with the Company. Only I wonder how *you'll* really like being in the *corps de ballet*?"

Drina frowned in silence until they reached Bedford Street, crossed it and headed for Chandos Place.

"What do you mean, exactly?"

"I should have thought it was obvious. You've been almost a star. You *were* a star in Francaster last Christmas, with your name in huge letters, and it was quite big even in Paris for Little Clara. In a kind of way it will be a step back for you. Now don't look cross. It's common sense."

"I'm not cross. I see what you mean, though I must say I'd never thought of it before. I still feel that just to be in the Company, the lowest member, will be enough."

"Yes, I know. I feel the same, of course. But you won't find it easy to fall into line."

"Then I shall worry about it when the time comes," Drina said sturdily …

It was well after five o'clock when Drina let herself into the flat and her grandmother appeared at once.

"There you are, Drina! I thought you'd hurry home after what must have been a very tiring day. How did you get on at the rehearsal?"

"Quite well, I think, Granny. Everyone seemed satisfied."

"You look tired, all the same. I wish you wouldn't try to do too much."

"I don't, Granny. I'm strong as a horse now."

Mrs Chester sighed.

"I'm sure I hope so. Well, take your things off and come and have some tea. There are two letters for you. I put them in your room. One is from New York."

Drina's heart leaped in a way that sent the colour to her face, but her grandmother had turned towards the living-room and didn't notice. From Grant? Would he have written so soon? He had suggested that she might write to him occasionally, but in all the long months between New York and Paris he had only sent her a card and Christmas present. She had steeled herself to another silence, but hope was quickly born.

The letter certainly bore a New York postmark, but it was from Yolande Mason, the girl whom Drina had met on the *Queen of the Atlantic*. The other was from Jenny Pilgrim, Drina's friend who lived in the Warwickshire town of Willerbury.

Drina stood looking down at Jenny's letter, feeling

vaguely worried and guilty. It was a great sadness to her that she and Jenny seemed to be drifting apart, for they had been very close for a number of years. But, where life had been kind to her, it had been very cruel to Jenny, who had had to give up her dearest hopes of going to an agricultural college at the time when her father went bankrupt. Now she was taking commercial subjects – something that she hated bitterly – and in a short time she would be leaving school to work in an office. Trouble and disappointment, and the brave effort to hide her feelings from her family, had altered Jenny, and she was no longer the happy, plump, always understanding friend.

It hurt Drina to think of Jenny now: a tall, slim, rather hard-eyed young woman who seemed much older than her years. Next month Jenny would be sixteen, but she might have been twenty by the way she talked. And, Mrs Chester might have said, not a very attractive twenty. For Drina's grandmother had been decidedly shocked by the change in Jenny, though she could not help admiring the grim courage with which she had tackled her unwelcome new life.

Jenny's letter was quite short, where once she would have written many cheerful pages.

Dear Drina,
How are you? Back from Paris now, I suppose, and tackling the new term at the Dominick. Some people have all the luck! Your cards of Montmartre and l'Opéra made me quite ill with envy. Drina had been afraid of this and had hesitated for quite a long time before sending the cards. *Life goes on here much as usual. I'm working hard at book-keeping, that wretched shorthand and typing and all the rest, including ordinary lessons. Soon, though, the Grossdale will be behind me and I shall be out at work. I do try not to grumble, because*

it's my own decision to leave school at sixteen. I insisted on it –
I felt I had to earn and be independent, and when Dad's friend
said I was sure of a job with him … Well, that's it.

I still go to Brookes's Farm most weekends and it helps to
keep me sane. These fantastic May days are nearly unbearable,
being cooped up doing something I loathe – with a lot of spotty
boys and silly girls. And the thought of an even stuffier office
for the rest of my life – Well! Do you think that people ever
stop being affected by the whole atmosphere of spring? I hope I
soon grow out of it.

Timothy and I still go out sometimes. He is the only really
intelligent boy in my class and we have something in common
as he's yearning for forestry. Most of them call him my
boyfriend; perhaps he is. But there's another one in the offing.
I've met up with Robert Hogden again. You remember him?
At Hogdens' Farm, next to Uncle's. My uncle and aunt have
gone to Australia now, and some people I don't know have
their farm. Brookes's is far nearer Willerbury, and Mrs
Brookes is glad to have me at weekends, but Robert says that if
I want a change I can always go and work at Hogdens'. I might
take him at his word, too.

I wonder when you and I shall meet? Your granny is not
very likely to want to lose you so soon after Paris, and I just
can't afford to get to London yet. But I wondered if I could
come for a few days at the end of July and the beginning of
August before I start work? Let me know. You are always
dashing off somewhere.

Philip was home for a few days over Easter. He's getting
very grand now that he's well on the way to being a doctor. I
told him to call and see you some time, so don't be surprised if
an elegant hunk of manhood arrives on the doorstep. He really
has quite an air about him, though he's pretty short of money.
He's not at all a scruffy student. He'll end up in Harley Street,
and what fun if you married him! Though you and he may
have other ideas.

Must dash. Sunday, so due at farm.
Lots of love,
Jenny

Yolande's letter was chatty and happy, for she was enjoying her life in New York. She lived with an aunt in a pretty little house near Washington Square and attended ballet classes at a school on Madison Avenue.

I was glad to get your postcard, she wrote. *Such a lovely one, too! Paris must have been beautiful in the spring. But New York is too. The trees are very bright green in the Square and last Saturday I was up in Central Park. There was a lot of pink and white blossom and the lakes were so blue. I stood and looked south to the midtown skyscrapers – like fairy towers – and thought how much you would like to see it all. On Sunday my aunt and I went over to Staten Island to visit friends and when we came back on the ferry at sunset Manhattan looked unbelievable. Sometimes I think it's the most beautiful place in the world and it seems strange that I ever dreaded coming here. I have a lot of friends now and Madame says my dancing is coming on. In fact, she seems very pleased.*

Of course I do think of England and I always read the British ballet magazines most carefully, every single word. Someone from my old school, the Lingeraux, sends them to me.

Though her grandmother was calling her, Drina stood on by the window, seeing not the River Thames and Lambeth Bridge, but New York as Yolande had described it. Yes, it was beautiful. For all its occasional squalor, and the garishness of Times Square and other places, Drina agreed with all her heart that it was the most beautiful city she had ever seen. No city she had ever seen had moved her so much as New York at night, from the top of the RCA Building; looking down on a million lights, at jewelled bridges and the shine on black water.

It was not only that she had fallen in love in New York; it had, strangely, seemed her own place since she had first ventured out of the hotel on that hot September morning.

She sighed and wandered into the living-room.

"Jenny wants to know if she can come and stay at the end of July," she remarked, as she accepted a cup of tea.

"Well, I suppose she can, if she wants to. She knows she's always welcome," said Mrs Chester. "She'll be getting a job about then, surely?"

"Yes, but she wants a change first, I expect."

"That poor girl!! Pitchforked out into the world when she's barely sixteen, with no money behind her."

"It happens to lots of girls," said Drina, rather sadly. "There are plenty at the Dominick who haven't any money. I often feel ashamed because I'm so lucky."

"Oh, of course. But Jenny expected something different, and, though I never approved of a girl going farming, she would have enjoyed college."

"Farming was the only thing for Jenny," Drina said, even more sadly.

"But are you sure you want her to come *then*? Your grandfather and I haven't made any plans, but you've generally got something in mind for your holidays. I wondered if you'd want to go back to Italy, to see your Italian grandmother and the Gardinos. And you haven't been farther south to see your other relatives yet. Don't you want to visit Rome and Perugia?"

"Yes, I'd love to go some day. And I long to see Antonia again. It seems so long since last August, when she was here. She goes to a new school now, in Switzerland, and I'd love to hear all about it. The only thing is that Hildegarde said something about my going to Germany to visit them. Dinkelsbühl, you know. It sounds lovely."

"Yes, it's very charming. You'd love it; you have such a romantic mind."

Drina ignored the slight taunt.

"Granny, you can still surprise me! I didn't know you'd ever been to Germany."

"I stayed in Munich once, when Betsy was dancing there. Well, why not leave Jenny for a while and see how things plan out?"

Drina was frowning fiercely down at her plate.

"Granny, I can't. Jenny must come when she wants to. I couldn't do anything else."

Mrs Chester said shrewdly:

"You've grown away from her. It does happen, even with the best of friendships. Must you have a bad conscience about it?"

"I wish I needn't. It's very uncomfortable. It isn't really quite that, anyway. I'm still fond of Jenny. It's – oh, circumstances. Not being able to meet often, and me feeling guilty because I'm lucky and she isn't. No, I'll go to Germany later in August, if Hildegarde really wants me to. Maybe I could fly to Munich and they could meet me there." And Drina glanced doubtfully at her grandmother, for so far she had never flown anywhere. After her daughter's death in a plane crash, Mrs Chester had been, not surprisingly, reluctant to fly.

"If that's what you want," Mrs Chester said grudgingly. "As usual you'll make up your own mind." But her glance softened as she looked at the sensitive, downbent face. Drina was loyal and honest and never likely to take life too easily. It would be better if she *could*, thought the woman who rather distrusted emotions.

"Have you got much homework?" she asked presently.

"Yes, a horrible lot. I'd better get down to it."

"I don't know when you'll do it once you're in the play."

"In the dressing-room when I'm not on, I suppose," said Drina, and wondered how successful that would be when the play was likely to take such a firm hold on her.

4

Bad News for Everyone

The next morning Drina again rehearsed at the theatre, and it was after twelve when she reached the Dominick. She was at once aware of an unusual atmosphere. The students queuing in the canteen were not laughing and calling to each other as they normally did.

She took her place at the end of a line waiting for soup, and found Meryl, a member of her class, just in front.

Meryl turned round and said in a low voice:

"Heard the news?"

Drina's heart leaped. Obviously it was really bad news. Her mind immediately conjured up several terrible possibilities. Mr Dominick was dead ... the Dominick Theatre had been burned down ... something awful had happened to the Company, maybe a train accident on the Continent, or all the scenery lost.

"No."

"The Dominick is doomed." Meryl's voice was hollow and heads were nodding all around.

"*Doomed*?" Drina repeated faintly. Bankruptcy flashed into her mind.

"Yes. After next spring we won't be in Red Lion Square any more –"

"Those who want soup get a move on, for heaven's sake!" cried the woman behind the counter.

Drina moved up dumbly, and, taking a piping hot plate, went towards the table where Rose, Ilonka, the twins, Hildegarde, a boy called Jan Williams, and several others, were sitting in heavy silence.

"She's as white as a sheet!" said Sue sympathetically.

Drina put down the plate and then sat down herself, looking from one grave face to another.

"If you want to know, I feel sick. What on earth made me take this tomato soup? What did Meryl mean? Why is everyone looking like this? What's *happened* to the Dominick?"

"It was in the paper," Rose said rapidly. "Just in one paper, the *Mail*. Mr Dominick said when he talked to us all at ten o'clock that somehow the news slipped out before they had a chance to tell us. We take the *Mail* and Dad read it out to me before I left. You know we've all remarked about how the area has changed? All the new buildings everywhere? Well, the lease is up at the end of next March and it won't be renewed. There'll be an office block where we are now."

"I don't believe it," said Drina. She had never doubted that the Dominick School would go on for ever, exactly as it was now. Every inch of the buildings was familiar and, though they were old buildings and in many ways very inconvenient, she was deeply attached to them. The Dominick School was part of life – it *was* life. Why, her mother's ballet shoes had been in the glass case in the hall for more than fourteen years; the Dominick itself had been there for very much longer than that. The classrooms, the studios, the dark cloakrooms, the bare patch of "garden", were permanent, indestructible.

"You'll *have* to believe it, I'm afraid," said Jan Williams, a sensible boy who was a special friend of Drina's. "We were all shattered. Rose wasn't the only one who saw that bit in the paper. Mr Dominick gathered the whole school together and explained. He and Miss Volonaise are very upset too."

"I *thought* he was going to tell me something yesterday," said Drina, on a high, rather gasping note.

This was unfortunate, for, in the unusual silence about her, her voice carried to Queenie at the next table.

Queenie spun round, with bright, angry eyes.

"Listen to Drina! As though Mr Dominick would tell *her* before the rest of us!"

"Oh, shut up!" Drina cried, on the verge of tears and shocked by the fact. "He *didn't* tell me."

'Yes, shut up," agreed Rose, with unusual courage, for she was afraid of Queenie. "We've enough to worry about without you being spiteful."

"Well, I like that!" Queenie was outraged. "It comes to something when a plumber's kid from Earl's Court can speak so rudely to Beryl Bertram's daughter!"

"Oh, shut up," said Jan. "Rose is right. And don't be such a snob!"

Queenie subsided, for she had early met her match in Jan, who would never put up with any nonsense. But she registered a black mark against Rose and vowed that she would make her pay for it later.

"Next March, you said?" Drina asked feebly, still not sure that the shameful tears were safely locked away. "But we – what will happen to us? Where shall we go? Where will the Company rehearse?"

At that moment Igor passed by, bearing a plate of stewed fruit and custard. He paused to lean over Drina.

"We'll get a fantastic new school."

"I don't want a fantastic new school!" said Drina

fiercely and voices echoed her words.

Igor looked faintly amused, as he balanced the plate. His father might be Director of the School and Company, but Igor had spent a good part of his life in Paris and it was not so very many terms since he had been new and rather unpopular. The Dominick would presumably belong to him some day, but he obviously felt no special affection for the present building.

"How like the English. Sunk so deeply into 'tradition'. Do you mean that you all prefer this smelly old basement to a fine new restaurant and properly lighted cloakrooms where the girls can see to powder their noses?"

"We mean just that," said Rose firmly. "It's no use laughing, Igor. It's tragedy. It's awful! Every other student in the school feels the same."

Igor solemnly bore a spoonful of fruit and custard to his mouth.

"I am grave. I am bent under the weight of tragedy –"

"Oh, go away, you wretched boy!" said Joan Meredith. She had never really met Igor until recently, but she was certainly not in awe of him because he was the Director's son and in a higher class.

Igor bestowed on her a sunny and particularly irritating smile. It was impossible to ruffle his dignity.

"I go to finish this somewhat painful meal. With the offensive drink that the English call coffee."

"No, wait, Igor!" cried Rose, plucking at the sleeve of his sweater. "Did *you* know? It wasn't a surprise to you?"

"But of *course* I knew. It's been in the air for a long time, though my father and Miss Volonaise hoped that the lease might yet be renewed. It will be expensive to build, and the Company is not so rich."

"But where is the new school to be?" Drina asked,

after Igor had gone to his place at a table crowded with older boys and girls.

"Over on the South Bank, not far from the Festival Hall. They've managed to find a site there, and I bet it will cost a bomb," said Jan.

Drina ate what little lunch she could manage in silence and the rest of the day passed miserably. Even the members of staff seemed upset and were more lenient than usual over absent-mindedness in class.

Drina was kept behind for a few moments to discuss her previous night's essay, so she descended the main staircase alone. When she was halfway down, Marianne Volonaise came into the hall from the square and stood looking up at her. She was a beautiful and elegant woman, who had once been a dancer, and Drina admired her enormously, as did every other member of the School. Miss Volonaise – Madam – was a remote figure to most of them, but, as in the case of Mr Dominick, Drina had got to know her, helped lately by the fact that Marianne Volonaise had known Elizabeth Ivory very well.

Drina promptly pressed herself to the side of the wide staircase, but Miss Volonaise waited at the bottom and signalled to her to come down.

"Good gracious, Drina! You look more miserable than most! Do you really mind so much?"

"I mind very much –" said Drina shakily, and could not go on.

"Well, it's a pity, and we're all upset, but things must change sooner or later and we certainly will have a far better and more convenient building. And I can promise you that your mother's portrait and ballet shoes will hang in the new hall."

Drina flushed.

"Oh, Madam, someone might hear!"

Marianne Volonaise laughed.

"You're still adamant about keeping it a secret?"

"Oh, yes. I – I couldn't bear everyone to know. They – they already think –" And she stopped abruptly, flushing even more deeply.

The joint Director of the School eyed her shrewdly, but asked no questions. It was not so very long since Drina had tried to get out of going to Paris because of remarks made by Christine Gifford. Inevitably there was much jealousy, especially when a girl proved herself very talented. Miss Volonaise hated the fact, but was forced, on most occasions, to accept it. Though Christine had been expelled for that and other misdemeanors.

"Well, look! Next March is still a long way off. Plenty of good things can happen before then. Cheer up, my dear! There are worse tragedies."

"Not to me. Or most of us. We – we like things as they are, whatever Igor says."

Igor's godmother laughed.

"I can guess what Igor said. He'll make himself unpopular again, silly boy. Well, run along and try not to take it too much to heart. And good luck in *Diary of a Dancer*. When do you start?"

"Tomorrow. It was to have been Thursday, but Giovanna really is bad and Mr Campbell says I'll be all right after a rehearsal in the morning."

"Then you've plenty to think about." She patted Drina's arm lightly and went on up the stairs and Drina went to the cloakroom, feeling, for the moment, a little comforted.

Mindful of her grandmother's remarks – and in any case feeling disinclined for any company, even Rose's – Drina made excuses to her friends and set off home.

Mrs Chester received her with relief that soon turned into alarm and indignation.

"Well, I'm glad you're early. But what's the matter? Why do you always come home looking so wrought up?"

"I don't, Granny. I was all right yesterday."

"You're not all right now. Well, out with it."

"Something *terrible* has happened!"

Mrs Chester chuckled.

"You always exaggerate so. I never know whether you really mean it."

Drina poured out the story of the Dominick and her grandmother listened attentively.

"Well, I can see that you're all sorry, but it isn't really so very tragic, now is it? You'll get a new building, and no doubt it's high time. The old one is pretty scruffy."

"It seems to me absolutely perfect," said Drina and went gloomily to her room, feeling that she would never come to terms with the knowledge that the Dominick, as they now knew it, would be gone in not much more than ten months' time.

But by the next evening the news about the Dominick had fallen more into perspective. After all, ten months was a very long time, and meanwhile, there was so much to occupy Drina's mind. Most of all the play, and the moment she reached the Queen Elizabeth Theatre she had no thoughts for anything else.

She was, for one thing, much more nervous than usual, and then it was always exciting to step back into the world of the theatre again. The whole atmosphere ... stage hands and electricians hurrying about ... the business of getting made up. And then the play itself, really important and moving.

There were a good many messages and cards to wish her good luck, and the only wandering thought she allowed herself was that Grant, in far away New York, did not even know that she was on in a West End play. One of these days she would pluck up courage to write to him and tell him the news.

"Overture and beginners, please."

The theatre, Carlotta had said, looking in on Drina a few minutes before, was packed to capacity, as it had been almost every evening since the play opened months ago. That was good news, but it was less reassuring to remember that there might be critics out there in front. They sometimes attended when there was a change of cast.

But all that really mattered was slipping once more into Ilonka's skin, the skin of the girl who had gone through this actual experience; the planning of the desperate escape from Lynzonia.

Drina was on at the very beginning of the play, before the whole family and their neighbour gathered to make the arrangements. The curtain rose to show her playing with Mitzi, while the room was filled with the sound of ballet music – the Black Swan *pas de deux* from the third act of *Lac des Cygnes*.

From then on Drina forgot the audience, everything. The play was reality, this time a reality into which she had stepped and had not helped to build up bit by bit through the early rehearsals. It was a living thing, tense with fear and anxiety and a thread of hope. Some day, perhaps, the Lorencz family might all be safe in London.

The first act ended, and the curtain came down on some moments of moved silence; always the greatest tribute to a production. Then the applause roared out. Drina stood dazed and lost, still clutching Mitzi, who made no protest, though Drina's grasp was not gentle.

Tonight there could be no thought of doing school work during the time when she was not on stage. Drina stood in the O.P. corner throughout the second act and the first part of the third, only leaving it to change into her coat and scarf for the scene when they arrived from the airport. It was draughty in the corner, but she did not even notice.

Her stage "mother" joined her and they made their entrance together. The scene went on ... the music from the off-stage production of *Swan Lake* swelled out ... Drina/Ilonka flung off her outdoor clothes and began to dance in her short, shabby dress, her face filled with hope.

The curtain came down and then rose again and again on the assembled cast. Drina bowed with the rest, but she was not really seeing the rows of faces and hearing the applause. She was still absorbed in the part, and it was not until she had removed her make-up and changed that the real world really impinged.

The doorman had called her a taxi, but first there were autograph books to be signed at the stage door.

"Why, you really are only a kid!" cried one voice.

Drina smiled and went on signing, then escaped to the taxi. It was Calum Campbell himself who put her into it.

"You were very good. Don't fear those terrible dragons, the critics."

"I'll try not to. Good night!" And Drina was borne away down Kingsway in the last of the sunset. It was keeping light late now and London looked clear cut and clean in the bright evening.

Tired, Drina sat back, and stared out. She felt drained, but contented, and the last guilty feelings about her original refusal to be in the play had gone. It might be a strain to act Ilonka every evening, but she knew she had done the right thing and was doing it to the best of her ability.

"I *am* so very lucky," she told herself, as they drove down Whitehall towards the dimming towers of Westminster. "I have everything. I suppose it can't go on for ever." And suddenly, though it was very warm, she shivered. In the weeks to come she was to remember that strange moment of fear; it was almost as though she had had a premonition.

5

June Days

For some time, however, life went on fairly peacefully; or, at any rate, as peacefully as it ever did for Drina. Even the dreaded critics were at their best, rather than their worst, for almost all those who had troubled to see the play again wrote in praise of the new Ilonka.

"Miss Drina Adams's performance in *Diary of a Dancer*," wrote one eminent man, "is extremely moving. It is not a long part, but it demands much from an actress who is still very young. One almost believes that Drina Adams herself suffered the pain and fear of being a refugee, so completely does she convince us. This is not a great play; it is, in some ways, slight in plot and action, but it amply makes up for these faults by its sustained atmosphere."

"Drina Adams took over ably from Giovanna Renti in *Diary of a Dancer* last night," wrote another. "No, it was something much more than ableness. Her performance was moving and utterly convincing. This young girl is, I believe, destined for the ballet. This may well be a loss for the straight theatre, for Miss Adams has proved more than once that she has more than average acting talent. Her last night's performance moved me almost to tears."

Mr Chester was quietly pleased over the comments

and carried the newspaper clippings to show to his friends. Mrs Chester read them all, too, but her remarks were entirely in character.

"Well, I'm glad you've done well. You've never before had such undiluted praise. But don't let it go to your head."

Drina laughed, rather shakily.

"Oh, Granny! You do try to keep me on the right road. I'm not conceited, am I?"

"No," said her grandmother, grudgingly. "It's a miracle, but you're not. You might be an insufferable child after all the publicity you've had during the past few years."

"I feel – oh, I truly feel humble about this play. I'm not me, I'm Ilonka. I'm all the girls like her who have lost their country. Does that sound smug? I don't mean it to. It's so hard to explain."

"It's clear enough. It *is* a moving play. But don't get mystic about it."

Mysticism would hardly flourish, Drina thought ruefully, in the everyday atmosphere created by her grandmother.

All the same, there were times during the following weeks when she looked at Ilonka almost with wonder. But Ilonka was now almost always cheerful and she had good reason to be, for she was happy at the Dominick, her dancing was good, and she had many friends.

Rose, on the contrary, was not nearly so contented. As she had feared, her early days at the Dominick were not easy, though she was helped by the presence of the twins, Hildegarde, Drina, and many other friends. Though she did not talk about it much, she badly missed the spaciousness of Chalk Green Manor in its beautiful setting of woods and hills. For Rose, the born Londoner, who had at first been bewildered and uneasy in the country, had learned to love the Chilterns and to take her freedom on the hills for granted. She thought often of the flowers that would now be out in that lovely chalk countryside and how she might have been walking and cycling when ballet classes and ordinary lessons were finished for the day.

The Manor was enormous, with plenty of room for all its students, and Rose's own home was shabby and cramped. The Conways were a loving, easy-going family, and it was one of Rose's greatest problems that she had to keep the irksomeness of so many things from her hardworking mother. It was tiresome to have to share a room with two younger sisters, for it was tiny and as different as possible from the spacious bedroom she had shared at Chalk Green, with its views over the valley to the opposite hills. Worse still, she found her father and mother narrow-minded and set in their ways after her own constant contact with the staff and students of many nationalities, and she was always having to curb her tongue during the crowded family meal-times.

She missed the good and wholesome country food, too, for she had grown away from a diet of fish and chips and other fried foods.

"I do feel an absolute beast," she confessed to Drina once. "I do love them. They're my family. And Dad is so kind and warm-hearted. But he says the most awful things without knowing they're awful. He's never been abroad, of course, or even met many people of other nationalities, and then he just sits glued to the 'telly' every night, lapping up everything. He said to me last night that he couldn't think why I was so set on earning a few miserable pounds in the Dominick Company when I might earn hundreds a week as a pop star or tap-dancer or something."

"So you might," said Drina. Rose had a fairly good voice and had sometimes amused her by singing pop songs in the style of some of the television idols.

"Well, I don't want to, then. I do think guilt is the most awful emotion!"

"Yes," agreed Drina. "I don't know where conscience comes from. It's all very hard on you."

"Maybe I shouldn't have gone to Chalk Green. I always knew it was giving me 'ideas'. I even find myself wondering how soon I can get a flat of my own. Of course, it will be years and years, but I would have an excuse. There really isn't room for all of us now we've all grown so."

"You're only fifteen," said Drina, who was often astonished by the way her friends were growing up. It had never crossed her mind that she might one day want a place of her own.

"Well, in the autumn I'll be sixteen."

At the Dominick itself Rose enjoyed the ballet and "character" classes, where she could easily hold her own, but was less happy about her school work. Another of her problems was that she had no quiet place where she could do her homework. If she shut herself in the bedroom, where there was no space for a proper table, she had to be finished before her younger sisters went to bed. In any case, they promised often to leave her in peace, but were always bursting in to look for something. Downstairs there was little more peace, for the television was in the living-room and there was usually much coming and going in the kitchen: neighbours dropping in for a chat or to borrow something. The only other room downstairs was used as a bedroom; there was no table there, either, and the light was bad. It was all very difficult.

At the Dominick, too, there was Queenie Rothington,

in the same class for everything and so unavoidable. Queenie had never liked Rose, in the first place because she was Drina's friend, and she never lost an opportunity to pick on her. Her methods were sometimes quite subtle, for, after the affair of Christine Gifford, Queenie was careful. But she had only to look long enough at Rose's shabby case or her worn shoes, for Rose to be painfully aware of the fact.

"Sometimes I could choke her!" she said fiercely. "I'm not the only shabby one, and I don't see that Dad's being a plumber is particularly funny. Where would the world be without plumbers, anyway?"

"Just ignore her," said Drina.

"I do. I try to, anyway."

"You're just as pretty as Queenie and quite as good a dancer. Better, actually. Queenie hasn't danced with the Company."

"That's partly what's getting to her," said Rose.

But there were compensations, for in many ways Rose's freedom was far greater now than it had been at Chalk Green. Her mother regarded fifteen and a half as almost grown up. At the same age she had been working in a factory and "going steady" with the boy she had later married. She would have welcomed local boys to the family circle and was often distressed because her daughter only seemed to meet "those odd boys who are going to be dancers". Rose argued often and fiercely that they were not odd at all, but neither of her parents was in the least convinced.

In a fit of bravado she invited Jan Williams home one weekend and the visit was an unexpected success, because Jan was sensible and down to earth, interested in soccer and old steam engines. As both of these happened to be Mr Conway's particular passions, Rose found her nose out of joint and heartily welcomed the fact.

When she saw Jan off at the local Tube station in the evening he remarked:

"I like your father. I wish I'd got one. He died when I was six."

But some of the good done by Jan's visit was almost immediately spoilt by an unlucky encounter with Igor. Rose and her mother were on a rare shopping trip to the West End one Saturday morning and came face to face with Igor walking along Piccadilly.

Igor wore an emerald green shirt and bright pink, baggy trousers. He was tall and startlingly handsome; strong, too. He was going to be a dancer of great athletic drive, with remarkable elevation, but the overall impression was very flamboyant. It was even more so, to Mrs Conway's mind, when Igor stopped and fluttered his long lashes at Rose.

"Good morning, my sweet Rose! My day is now made."

"Don't be a fool, Igor!" said Rose uneasily. She introduced them and Igor shook hands and smiled in his most winning way.

"It's such a pleasure to meet you, Mrs Conway. Rose and I are great friends, aren't we, Rose?"

"Sometimes," said Rose brusquely. She could have kicked him, right there amongst the Saturday morning crowds in Piccadilly.

She dragged her mother away, muttering:

"You don't have to take any notice of Igor. He's always showing off. It comes of being Mr Dominick's son."

"Oh, is he the boy who grew up in *Paris*?" asked her mother, as though that amply explained some, at least, of Igor's idiosyncrasies. Though basically a kind woman, she made a good story of the encounter at the next family meal-time, and Rose writhed, but was powerless to say much more.

Drina, meanwhile, had a few problems of her own. She was so afraid of falling behind with her work that she was studying perhaps harder than she had ever done before, and this – coupled with her nightly performances at the Queen Elizabeth Theatre – often made her feel very tired. Any such feeling had to be kept from her grandmother, so she made an extra effort to be cheerful at home. Mrs Chester was not really deceived – she had not watched Drina growing up without knowing every nuance of her moods – but she did not say much. She merely insisted on Drina having a long lie-in on Saturday and Sunday mornings and dosed her with vitamin pills prescribed by the doctor.

Drina herself found Queenie's constant presence trying, though she had advised Rose to ignore the girl. She and Queenie would always be rivals and the fact was there all the time. If Drina's dancing was praised, Queenie scowled and tried to draw attention to herself … if Drina was criticized over anything, or got poor marks in class, Queenie beamed and did not trouble to hide her delight.

But almost worse than Queenie was her cousin Sylvia. The early antagonism between Drina and Sylvia had developed until it was almost, Drina sometimes felt, a tangible thing. Sylvia was a showy but also a technically excellent dancer and she was used to being very much to the fore. She resented perhaps even more than Queenie did Drina's past and present successes.

Sylvia was clever, too, and had soon climbed almost to the top of the class. Then one week she was top, the next week Drina, and the week after that they both tied. This would not have mattered in the least if they had been friends, or even ordinarily friendly. But Drina found the rivalry painful and if she had not felt that she so vitally needed good marks she might almost have been tempted to slack and let Sylvia win.

Sylvia, she was rather horrified to learn, irritated her so much that there were times when she could hardly bear to be in the same room with her. Sylvia was always talking about herself. She often came out with such remarks as:

"When I was learning ballet in Milan I was quite the star of my class. They said I was good enough to dance at La Scala."

Or:

"Really the Dominick has nothing on my ballet school in New York. There they really knew the meaning of teaching."

She was extremely scornful over the sorrow felt about the doomed building, and even Queenie was moved to expostulate on one occasion.

"Yes, but, Sylv, you've only just come. You can't be expected to feel as we do."

"It's just nothing but sentimentality," said Sylvia once, overhearing some remark of Drina's, and Drina's hand positively itched to slap her pretty, arrogant face. Sylvia, seeming to know this, gave her a long, considering, anything but friendly look, then laughed and turned away with a careless:

"Of course, some of you girls are really very young for your age. In America girls are far more *developed*."

She was not generally popular, as might be imagined, but, like Queenie, she had her admirers.

With so much dancing, school work and the play, there

was not much time for anything else. There was scarcely even time for thinking about Grant. Drina sometimes promised herself that she would think about him when she got to bed, but she almost always fell asleep at once. She did write to him, but found the letter unexpectedly difficult. She longed to pour out some of her feelings but knew that she just could not do so. Grant liked her, she was sure of that, but he was several years older and he might well have told himself, as soon as the days in Paris were over, that the whole thing was best forgotten, at least for the time being.

So in the end she sent him a rather short letter, with details of the main news, and even ran into trouble when she came to end the letter. Should she say, "With love from Drina"? Or just "Yours, Drina"? Or what? At last she rather defiantly scrawled "Love from Drina", thrust the thin sheets into the airmail envelope and wrote the address: "Mr Grant Rossiter, Central Park West, New York, 10023, N.Y., U.S.A."

Central Park West! She sat with the letter in her hand, remembering that evening when she and her grandparents had first gone to the Rossiters' apartment for dinner. She had stood by Grant in the darkened front room, gazing southwards to that beautiful view of the midtown skyscrapers at night, shining with lights; fairy towers against the darkened sky. In many ways it seemed the most unlikely thing in the world that she had ever stood there. New York ... it seemed a lifetime away, and yet every detail was still clear in her mind ...

Drina was so busy that for three weeks after returning from Paris she did not even go to see her friend, Adele Whiteway. She and Rose had been with Miss Whiteway in Paris, and it was to Miss Whiteway, on that night when she said goodbye to Grant after the ballet at l'Opera, that Drina had spoken about him. Rose had guessed a good deal, but it was not a thing that Drina could speak of easily, even to a friend.

Then one Sunday she did go to Miss Whiteway's flat and found her putting the finishing touches to some costume designs. For Adele Whiteway, a dancer until an accident put an end to her career, was now well known as a designer of ballet scenery and costumes.

She seemed delighted to see Drina, but surveyed her anxiously.

"Well, you *are* a stranger! No, I don't in the least blame you. I know you've been very busy. And I've seen you in the play. I went last week. I thought you were excellent – better than Giovanna. But what have you been doing to yourself? Where has your Paris tan gone?"

"It just faded away," said Drina, curling up on the comfortable sofa. "I haven't had much time for going out."

"You look rather tired. That play must take it out of you, and you have your dancing and school work as well. Not miserable, are you?"

Drina did not attempt to misunderstand the question. She answered honestly:

"No. I feel much better than I did before Paris. Seeing him again, and getting to know him better, did help. And I've got it firmly in my mind that I'm too young and that dancing is more important. Just sometimes it comes over me in a wave ... how much I miss him, and what I'd give to hear his voice again. His voice more than anything. If Granny wouldn't think me quite mad, I believe I'd telephone New York."

"She would think it odd, I'm afraid, and it would cost a great deal to talk for long."

"Well, I'm earning plenty of money," said Drina sadly, "but I don't get it. Granny keeps me rather short,

I sometimes think. She doesn't believe in teenagers having money to throw about. It's one of her pet theories. There are times when I shall be glad to be grown up and then I can telephone the ends of the earth if I feel like it."

"Never mind. You'll see him again. Didn't he say he might come to London?"

"Yes, but not for ages. In some ways life seems to race, and in other ways it simply crawls. A year is so long, and it will be more than that."

"When do you come out of the play?"

Drina frowned.

"I don't know. Giovanna isn't better. She more or less collapsed and the doctor isn't pleased with her. Granny's mad, but it looks as though I shall be in until the end of June, at least."

"One can see her point."

"Oh, yes, though other girls do it. But Granny says I've got to be free before the Dominick exams: She's *even* written to Mr Campbell. I feel rather an idiot about that."

"Still, she's right. And I suppose there's an understudy?"

"Oh, yes, Janet Smith. She's quite nice, but she isn't very experienced and they don't seem keen to use her."

"At the end of term you'll need a proper holiday. What are your plans?"

"Oh, well, Jenny's coming for about ten days when we break up. Then in the middle of August I'm hoping to fly to Germany. There's a girl I used to know at Chalk Green who's come to the Dominick for a term. Hildegarde's told me all about Dinkelsbühl and I know it's going to be great. Another thing I'm trying to fit in is learning some German. Grandfather bought me some records and Hildegarde helps occasionally. She comes to tea sometimes."

"Well, that oughtn't to be hard for you. You already speak good French and Italian. It seems you have a gift for languages."

"It's fun. I love languages. And German *is* quite easy."

On the way home Drina thought about Germany. Hildegarde had certainly given her a wonderful picture of Dinkelsbühl, and its walls and towers and shining, swan-haunted moat, its ancient houses and its old cobbled streets with ornate fountains.

August seemed a long way off, but she was looking forward very much to that holiday.

So the weeks passed and for some time London lay under the most perfect June weather. The roses were full out in the parks and people wore bright clothes.

"Summer!" thought Drina contentedly, on the occasions when she felt the sun on her bare arms and legs. "Lovely summer!"

It was certainly a million times better than the long months of winter: standing in bus queues in the sleety rain, and her body, stiff with cold, taking so much longer to relax during ballet classes. Drina hated the cold and the wet, perhaps more than most people, maybe as a result of her Southern Italian blood.

But perfect weather never lasts long in England, so halfway through June the temperature dropped sharply and it began to rain with a steady persistence that was very disheartening. For several days Drina awoke to see wet pavements and a grey river, and it was necessary to get out warm sweaters and stronger shoes again.

Mr Chester got very wet one day and was unable to change into dry clothes for some time. The result was a bad cold, which worried Mrs Chester very much, for he had a weak chest and had never been very strong. Her worst fears were realised when the cold went on his chest and he developed a wracking cough. The flat grew a much quieter place, the doctor came every day, and anxiety made Mrs Chester short-tempered.

Drina, anxious herself, crept about and gave all the help she could, which was not much, as she was out most of the day.

Then came an afternoon when a small junior entered the classroom to say that Drina Adams was wanted on the telephone in the office.

With a leaping heart, and a feeling of sickness, Drina ran along the corridors, and heard her grandmother's controlled voice, but much more strained than usual, saying:

"You had better ask if you may come home early, Drina. I thought you'd want to know. The doctor has just been and he's arranging for your grandfather to go into hospital."

"Oh, but, Granny –!" Drina caught her breath. "Is he very bad?"

"Yes, I'm afraid so. It's turned to pneumonia. Hurry, dear, if you want to see him before he goes."

Drina put down the receiver and walked blindly back to her classroom to ask permission to leave.

6

Drina's Dark Time

Drina had never realised just how fond she was of her grandfather until then. He was a quiet man, and he had always left most decisions to his wife, but he had been an anchor in Drina's life, always willing to listen and to try to understand, always so pleased by her success.

Grandfather! she thought, in deepest panic and, permission received, she bolted down to the cloakroom for her outdoor clothes.

When she reached Kingsway, splashing through the puddles, an empty taxi was just coming towards her, and she hailed it at once. Buses were too slow in such an emergency and, fortunately, she had money with her.

The comparatively short journey seemed endless and her thoughts were terrible company. Her vivid imagination that could be such a curse showed her all the most terrible things ... her grandfather dying ... her grandfather dead.

She hardly knew how she got out of the taxi, paid the fare, and went up in the lift. The front door was ajar and her grandmother was waiting in the hall, wearing her outdoor clothes. She looked so white and shrunken that she was suddenly an old woman. Drina felt ten times more frightened than before.

But before she could say more than a few hesitant words the lift was up again and some men appeared carrying a stretcher and blankets.

"Just go and say goodbye. Don't upset him," said Mrs Chester tersely, and turned to greet the ambulance men.

Drina slipped into her grandfather's room and stood looking down at the bed. He, too, looked … he looked dreadful. But he gave her a faint smile and took her hand. His fingers were hot and dry.

"I'm sorry, Drina. Did you … have a fright? I'll be better – in hospital. Your grandmother can't cope with this. Look after her, won't you?"

"Yes. Oh, yes."

There seemed nothing more that she could say. She bent and kissed him and then withdrew, shrinking away from the ambulance men. Mrs Chester found her in her room, standing motionless, still in her outdoor things.

"I'm going with him, Drina. I've written the telephone number on the pad. But I expect I shall be back soon. They won't let me stay long. Now don't worry too much. They'll look after him. There are such wonderful drugs nowadays."

"Oh, Granny!" cried Drina. There was a vast lump in her throat.

Mrs Chester patted her arm.

"Have a cup of tea and get a meal ready for us. We've still got to eat, I suppose."

Then they had all gone and Drina obeyed in a daze, though she didn't want the tea and felt that she would never eat again. The rain dripped down outside the windows and mist lay low over the river. The days of hot sun and full-blown roses seemed very far in the past.

It was just after half-past three when she had arrived home and the time seemed to drag unbearably. Four-thirty came and then five o'clock. Drina had almost unconsciously snatched up her case with most of her homework in it and she tried to work. The electric clock made a strange noise now and again, but the London sounds were far away. Only Big Ben boomed almost into her ears, it seemed.

Five-thirty … she heard the lift stopping and flew to the door. Her grandmother was just shutting the lift. There were drops of rain on her shoulders and her smart hair-do was slightly untidy.

"I'm sorry; they were some time settling him and then they let me sit by him for a while. Drina, you look terrible!"

Drina might well have answered, "So do you!" She was shocked by her grandmother's face. Its very composure was somehow more dreadful than tears and openly expressed sorrow might have been.

"He really is in good hands, and they seem very hopeful. Only, of course, he's never been strong. I wish now that we'd moved away from the river … too damp, perhaps … too many fogs. But he liked it. He always loved the Thames."

The fact that she spoke in the past tense frightened Drina so much that she could not say a word.

They ate an unwanted meal mainly in silence and by the time they had washed up it was almost time for Drina to go to the theatre. She said with difficulty:

"I'll telephone them. I won't go. Janet can go on."

But that Mrs Chester would not allow.

"No, indeed. You've got your job to do and it will be better for you. Mrs Willis will come up and keep me company. She's a kind soul and not one of your ghoulish people. I'll be all right with her, so you needn't worry."

In a way it *was* better to be doing something. Drina felt sick in the taxi, but composure came as she entered the stage door. After all, people didn't often die of pneumonia nowadays. There *were* wonderful drugs and he had gone to one of the best hospitals in London.

Her white face brought some inquiries and she explained briefly that her grandfather was ill. Warm sympathy nearly unsettled her again, but there was not too much time.

She had to change and get made up … she had to remember the play.

The next morning she tried to get out of going to school, but her grandmother was adamant. The news was not all that bad … Mr Chester was very ill, but had had a fair night. What good would it do for her to be mooning round the flat?

"I might keep you company," said Drina, with a gasp.

Mrs Chester's face softened.

"Yes, of course. But I shall be going to the hospital – they said I could go this afternoon. And I've a lot of telephoning to do and things to see to. You go to school. If I want you, I can telephone."

Drina spent a dreadful day, waiting for a summons that did not come. Now, in her grief and fright, everything else seemed small and mean and Queenie and Sylvia hardly seemed real. Queenie, in fact, even said that she was sorry to hear about Drina's grandfather. She was not really bad or heartless, only arrogant and overbearing, and she had not been helped by her parents, who were rather hard people, respecting only wealth and success. Drina triumphant Queenie could not abide, but Drina looking so white and pinched was enough to upset anyone.

Drina's friends rallied round her, but their sympathy seemed to come from a long way off. Once she thought:

"This must be a nightmare. I shall wake up."

But she didn't, and in a clearer moment she thought:

"It's happened to other people. I remember Bella once when her mother was ill in Italy. But how *shall* I bear it if he dies?"

For two days there was little change. The hospital bulletins were rather guarded and Mrs Chester grew quieter and quieter, her face so white and set that the whole bone structure showed clearly.

Drina never knew how she carried on as usual, but her grandmother saw that she did. Then came the afternoon when the news was worse.

Drina returned home from school to find her grandmother in her outdoor clothes, a small case in her hand.

"I have to go, Drina. He's very bad. They've tried everything ... I don't know ... I may have to stay the night. If I do, I'll telephone Mrs Willis and she will expect you after the theatre."

Fear seemed an all-possessing thing, then.

"Granny," Drina got out, after struggling for a few moments, "let me come, too. I've got to go with you!"

"No, my dear. They wouldn't let you. You couldn't do anything. He wouldn't know you."

The years of discipline made it impossible to cry or storm; Drina couldn't have done it under that controlled gaze. Even in the midst of direst trouble Mrs Chester would have despised helpless emotion.

"Then I shall stay here. I can't act; how *could* I? No one would expect it of me. I – I love him, too."

Mrs Chester said in a voice that was cold with strain:

"I know you do, but I think you must go to the theatre. Isn't that something you must learn? It may be

nonsense to say that the show must go on, but – Betsy danced when her husband, your father, was dying. It nearly killed her, too, but she danced. She said that people expected to see her. Betsy had courage."

"I – I don't think that *I* have any."

The girl and the woman stood eyeing each other, and Drina thought with a rush of feeling that she wished her grandmother were different. Warmer ... more sympathetic. Mrs Chester was broken-hearted, almost at the end of her tether, but she would never let that make any difference.

She turned away from Drina saying harshly:

"You've chosen the theatre, haven't you? It's a hard master."

"Does she hate me?" Drina thought, and then her grandmother turned back again to kiss her briefly.

"I didn't mean that. It will be better for you to go. You can't help me tonight."

Then she had gone and Drina flung herself down and cried until she could hardly see. That, suddenly was the worst thing of all, that she could not help her grandmother. She knew it to be true. Her grandmother loved her husband perhaps all the more because she found any emotion so hard to express. They had spent a good part of their lives together and not even the beloved granddaughter could help at what might be the moment of parting.

"But he can't, he can't, he can't die!" wailed Drina into a cushion. "I *do* love him, too. And I haven't any courage."

But she had. She washed her face and got herself a meal that almost choked her, and later set off for the theatre. "Betsy danced when your father was dying ..." Did the theatre really demand that?

She could think of innumerable instances. People

didn't *always* appear when a tragedy struck very near them, but very often they did. It might be wrong, it might be cruel or unnecessary or even downright silly, but they did it. They went on stage with broken arms ... with high temperatures ... when they were nearly dying themselves.

"But I shouldn't mind if *I* were dying!"

Her grandmother's words echoed and re-echoed in Drina's head on her way to the theatre.

"You chose the theatre ... it's a hard master ... I didn't mean that."

But Mrs Chester *had* meant it. She had expressed, then, some of the deeply rooted resentment she had always felt against the world that both her daughter Betsy and her granddaughter had chosen.

"I hope – if Grandfather ever knows – that he understands why I've come here tonight," thought Drina. But she knew that he would understand; he had never failed her when it came to the test, though at times in the past he had allowed his wife to make the important decisions.

Drina remembered that nightmare evening until the end of her life. It taught her much about herself and about her grandmother, and it also taught her that life just had to go on when, for someone she loved, it might be ending.

She was told afterwards that her performance was even better than usual; perhaps some of her own unhappiness and fear went into her portrayal of the refugee child from Lynzonia. But at the end she scarcely waited for the last fall of the curtain to dash away and be sick: the result of strain and badly-digested food.

Carlotta found her, white and shaking, trying to remove her make-up.

"Drina, there's a message for you at the stage door.

It's good news, so stop looking like that.''

Drina flew, in her pink housecoat, disregarding a few curious faces that looked in from the side street. The message had been telephoned half an hour before by her grandmother.

"Your grandfather is sleeping. The worst is over and they think he'll be all right. I'll be home when you get there."

"Thank God! Oh, thank God!" Drina thought. She felt utterly drained and weary.

She left by way of the front of the theatre and drove home through the wet, dim evening. She felt very little just then; she was only dimly conscious that the nightmare was over.

7
The End of Term

From then on she felt very close to her grandmother, for Mrs Chester's iron control had softened once she knew the danger to be past. But the memory of that terrible evening remained to trouble Drina deeply: she just could not forget it.

A week later, while her grandfather was still in hospital, she came out of the play, for Giovanna was well enough to take over the role again. Drina was glad. She had done what she had felt to be her duty, and in a strange way had even enjoyed being in *Diary of a Dancer*, but it was a relief to know that now her evenings would be free for school work and perhaps a little relaxation.

She went to see Adele Whiteway after school on the day after her part in the play ended. Adele, who knew all about the worrying time, was privately horrified by Drina's white and drawn appearance, but made no comment. She merely provided tea and chocolate biscuits and sat down by the open window to listen.

"You are a – a sort of father confessor, aren't you?" Drina asked shakily.

Adele Whiteway paused. Drina was not the only one who brought her confidences and asked for advice.

"If it helps you to talk, I'm glad to listen. But your grandfather's better, isn't he?"

"Nearly. He's coming out of hospital in a day or two. Of course he'll have to be very careful, but we aren't so terribly worried any more."

"Then –?"

After a few moments it all poured out.

"I can't forget – it was important, somehow. She didn't want me. I couldn't help. She didn't even – even seem really to remember that I – that I loved him, too. There was a moment when she seemed to hate me. She *made* me go to the theatre. She said I'd chosen it and it was a hard master. Almost at once she said she hadn't meant it, but she did. Doesn't she love me at all?"

"How has she been since then?"

"Oh, nicer than almost ever before. We've – we've seemed close, and we've gone to the hospital together to see him. But when it most mattered –" Her voice shook.

Adele Whiteway said slowly:

"No, of course she doesn't hate you. She loves you very deeply. But she loves your grandfather more. And you must always remember the type of woman she is – so self-contained and rigidly controlled that worry is bound to make her more so. You are very different. You seem to have far more Italian blood than Chester blood and she's always resented it. Though, in actual fact, your mother was a Chester also and she had a warm and outgoing personality. Mrs Chester always resented Elizabeth's great fame; she thought – wrongly, as it happens – that it spoilt her marriage and made her less of a human being. She resented seeing so comparatively little of Elizabeth and, most of all, the fact that her dancing was the direct cause of her death. You know all this, anyway. She fought to take you, and she vowed that on no account should you go near the theatre or the world of ballet, and what happens? You, at five years old or so, were inexplicably interested in dancing. At nine or ten you knew what you wanted. It must have been the bitterest possible thing for her to bear."

"Oh, but –"

"You fought, you were obstinate, you developed great individuality and you beat her to a standstill. By the time you were thirteen you were acting in a West End play and dancing, too. She had to give in to it all – she had no choice – but she's never wholly been resigned. She loves you, but she wishes that you were different. She's never quite known how it happened, when you were always subject to her influence –"

"I do know all that. But I couldn't help any of it. Do I have to feel guilty?"

"*No.* Of course not. People must develop their own way. Anything else would be unthinkable. But in a moment of great stress and agony that remark slipped out. She did mean it. You *did* choose the theatre and it is a hard master. But it's only a bit of the story so far as she's concerned. She most certainly loves you deeply. You'll just have to learn to understand how she feels."

"I do really."

"Then try to forget that evening. It will do no good to remember it. Forgiveness is a hard lesson to learn, but we all have to learn."

"I do forgive her. It – it wasn't really that."

"The whole thing was terrible for you, especially at a time when you had so much else to cope with. And you've the end of term examinations just ahead. I think you should get out as much as possible."

Mrs Chester echoed the words a few days later, when Mr Chester was home and well on the way to convalescence.

"You look like a ghost, Drina. It's time you had some fun. Why don't you and Rose book for Covent Garden?

And do get out on Saturdays and Sundays."

So Drina and Rose did go to the Royal Opera House one Saturday evening, and it was remarkably good to be back. They went in the amphitheatre, since Rose could not afford more expensive seats, and both were thrilled with *Antigone*. Drina adored the music, by a Greek composer, finding in it much that was strange, exciting and deeply moving.

"It's so modern and yet so – so ancient," she said later. "That music after the battle ... I thought it was superb."

They also saw *Danses Concertantes* and *Pineapple Poll*, and certainly the last was very attractive and amusing. As the great red and gold curtain came swishing down at the very end, Rose sighed:

"We *must* come more often! There's nowhere like the Garden."

"All the same," said Drina. "I always think that *Danses Concertantes* is exactly the sort of ballet that would put people off if they weren't very keen. This is the third time I've seen it and I must admit it doesn't do much to me. And I remember what Grandfather said once – of course he doesn't like ballet, really. But he was very funny about it, especially about the men."

The Dominick Company was touring in the provinces, but they went to see a foreign ballet company another Saturday, and Ilonka, Jan and Drina went to a concert at the Royal Festival Hall one Sunday.

The weather was better again so Drina and Rose sometimes walked on Hampstead Heath, and once, when he was feeling stronger, Mr Chester drove them out to the Chilterns. He and Mrs Chester spent a peaceful afternoon sitting in the sun and reading, while Drina and Rose ran eagerly up the drive of Chalk Green Manor.

It seemed so long since either had been in the

country. All the students of their own age had left the Manor now, but they had friends amongst the younger ones and Drina was particularly glad to see Jan's cousin, Bronwen. It was good to see the members of the staff, too, and Petrouchka, the little mongrel dog, had by no means forgotten either of them. In fact, he gave Drina, especially, a violent and rapturous welcome, for Petrouchka, even though such a long time had passed, never forgot that Drina had been his rescuer and first mistress.

Later they wandered alone along the Icknield Way, exclaiming over flowers and the familiar trees of the chalk country: spindle, the wayfaring tree, dogwood and wild privet. They sat at the edge of a silvery barley field just below the hidden white splash of Bledlow Cross, with the great cloud shadows sweeping over them, and Drina lay back, turning her face to the sky.

"Oh, Rose, this is so wonderfully peaceful! I do love this country. Sometimes I think I would choose it before anywhere else."

"Before New York?" Rose asked slyly.

"But New York is a *city*. I do love cities, and you know I adore New York. But the Chilterns have something I've never found anywhere else. Quiet and secret, but so beautiful."

They all needed what fun and peace they could snatch, for the end of the summer term at the Dominick was a worrying time, with exams and medical inspections. The school doctor frowned over Drina and did not seem very pleased.

"Have you been working too hard?"

"No," said Drina, in a panic. "Not really. We had problems ... it's over now. My grandfather was very ill."

"Well, you need a holiday. Forget dancing and

everything else."

"But I must practise!"

"Not even that for a little while. Get out and enjoy yourself. Don't worry about anything."

Rose fared better, but reported rather shamefacedly that she had been asked about her diet.

"I *can't* convince Mum that I eat too many fried things. We've always had them. It's not a bit of good talking."

Drina hated some of the examination papers, especially the maths one, for she was not good at figures. But her despair was lightened when she got home by finding a note from Grant, with some newspaper clippings about New York events. This was the second note he had sent her; one had come during the dark days of her grandfather's illness and she had carried it in her handbag ever since.

Things go on much the same here, Grant wrote. *It's very hot now and I look forward to my vacation. I'm flying over to the west coast to visit some relatives near San Francisco. I guess you're still working hard at the Dominick, but your German trip sounds as though it will be kind of fun.*

I wish I could have seen you in that play. He ended, as before, with: *My best, always. Yours, Grant.*

Drina felt that life was wonderful for quite a time afterwards.

There was also a letter from Yolande by the same post.

I love the heat, she wrote, *and I don't even really mind the humidity. But my aunt says we must get away from the city for a few weeks, if she can leave the shop. We may go to stay with a friend of hers – it's on the hills above Albany and sounds lovely – and then maybe to the coast of Maine.*

How is London? I often think of it. Last week the girl who lived next door to me, and who is in the Lingeraux Ballet Company (the youngest member), sent me some clippings and their summer program – Yolande was always now using American spelling *– and they're having quite a time. The Company has already danced in Italy and Israel this summer and halfway through August they're going to Madeira, for a little Festival that's going to be held in Funchal. It often seems odd to me that I might one day have danced with the Lingeraux. They're not as good or as big a company as the Dominick, but good enough and they do some interesting things.*

Thank you for the clippings you sent and all your news. I do want to keep in touch.

Love from
Yolande

Just before the end of term Mr Chester broke the news that he was retiring. He had never been back to work since his illness and Drina had suspected as much. It was not really a shock, but all the same she felt worried. He still looked old and a little feeble, though he seemed cheerful enough.

"I sometimes think we may move from Westminster," she said to Rose. "And I shall be sorry. I hated it at first – how long ago that seems! I wasn't quite twelve when we left Willerbury. But now I do love it."

When the examination results came out Drina had taken a high place, in spite of the maths paper, and Sylvia had done even better.

"But she wouldn't have done if *you* hadn't had so much to worry you," Rose said indignantly.

"Well, I don't care. She's as pleased as anything and I shan't see her again until September."

Drina was glad that the term was almost over. It had

been a strain in very many ways and she was particularly looking forward to the trip to Germany. She said goodbye to Hildegarde on the last day of term, with the knowledge that they would meet again in three weeks' time.

"It will be such fun to show you everything," said Hildegarde. She felt sad because her short time at the Dominick was over and it was a wrench to leave old and new friends.

Drina, Rose and Ilonka walked towards Piccadilly for the last time for nearly seven weeks. It was a hot July afternoon and the streets were dusty. They were all in high spirits, though Ilonka was only having a few days' holiday with her mother: Mrs Lorencz felt that she could not leave the restaurant for long. Rose and her family were going to a farm in Kent for ten days.

"I'm looking forward to it," she said. "But it did make me feel bad to listen to so many of the others. The twins and their cruise, and Queenie and Norway – what a fuss she made about it! You would think that no one else ever goes anywhere. It's the most usual thing for Dominick pupils to fly all over the world, but I must admit I shall never get used to it."

They walked as far as the narrow lane that led to the Golden Zither and there said goodbye to Ilonka.

"Are you in a hurry, Drina?" asked Rose.

"Well, I suppose I *should* hurry. But Granny will understand as it's the end of term."

"Then let's go and sun ourselves in Green Park for ten minutes."

They crossed Piccadilly and walked over the grass to a part of the park where there were not so many people. They flung themselves down and lay there for several minutes in silent contentment, hearing the muted sounds of traffic in the distance and the laughter and voices of children playing.

"I wish summer needn't ever be over," said Drina at last.

"Well, there's plenty left of it yet. The holidays have only just this minute started."

"I know. And Jenny will be here the day after tomorrow."

As she went home a short while later Drina was thinking of Jenny. They would have ten days together – the longest they had managed for some time – and Jenny just *must* enjoy herself. For her the holidays would not last long.

Big Ben was striking half-past five as Drina reached Parliament Square and she quickened her pace almost to a run. The term was over – goodness knew what the future would bring. But it was good to be free.

BOOK TWO
Ballet in the Sun

1
New Plans

The next morning Drina was awake early and she lay thinking about the coming visit to Germany. Loving travel as she did, the thought of seeing a new country was an increasing thrill and she had already built up a series of pictures in her mind: Hildegarde and her parents meeting her at the airport ... the drive to Dinkelsbühl along the Romantic Road ... the little fairy-tale city in the corn-gold fields, remote and almost untouched throughout the centuries.

Whenever she thought of the actual flight, Drina's heart seemed to leap, for she was far more nervous about it than she would ever have admitted. It had been a surprise that her grandmother had agreed so easily after all her past prejudice, and Drina had told herself over and over again that everyone flew nowadays and the fact that her mother had died in a plane accident could not put her off such an easy mode of travel for the rest of her life. For one thing, ballet companies flew all over the world, and if she became a member of the Dominick and they danced, say, in China, it would be impossible to go by sea or overland. Once she had actually experienced a flight she would probably love it, but the first time would be both exciting and frightening.

But before that would come Jenny's visit and Drina

was increasingly sad to realise how little she was looking forward to that. Last time it had been quite a while before they were at ease together and she did not expect things to be any better on this occasion.

These thoughts were so uncomfortable that she rose and had a bath, then dressed slowly, deliciously aware that there was no need to hurry. When she arrived at the breakfast table both her grandparents were halfway through the meal, but Mrs Chester said indulgently:

"I'm glad you didn't hurry. I was going to bring your breakfast to you in bed."

"Thank you, Granny, but I was too wide awake to stay there," said Drina, and was dimly aware, as she accepted fruit juice, that there was an even larger pile of mail than usual beside her grandfather's plate. He had an abstracted air, too, but then he had often seemed absent-minded lately. Perhaps he was sad about his retirement. Drina realised guiltily that she had not really thought much about his feelings, especially during the last days at the Dominick.

Now, eating her boiled egg, she suddenly sensed that there was something in the wind. They were both watching her and there was a slightly tense atmosphere. She finished her breakfast uneasily and then helped to clear the table. When the two of them were alone in the kitchen with the door shut, Mrs Chester said:

"I'm afraid I've a disappointment for you, Drina."

Drina stood frozen, with her hand on the tap. So there *was* something! And probably a big something. She knew all the tones of her grandmother's voice and this one was grave and rather apologetic.

"What is it, Granny?"

"Were you looking forward very much to going to Germany?"

With water splashing over the dirty dishes Drina glanced round at her grandmother, who was holding a tea-cloth and looking at her seriously.

"Yes, yes. I – I am. Was." The past tense used by her grandmother seemed at once to wipe the proposed visit right out of life. At once all her dream pictures faded away and it was a bitter moment, for she had not yet learned to take disappointment philosophically.

"I'm very sorry," said Mrs Chester evenly. "Very sorry indeed. You must believe me. But you can go some other time, and Hildegarde will understand."

"But what *is* it, Granny?" Drina was frightened now as well as disappointed. "Grandfather isn't still ill, is he?"

"No, not really, though he's far from strong. The doctor said a few days ago that he really must have a holiday in a warm place – a holiday and a real rest. And I think that you should come with us. Your grandfather," she added, with some reluctance, "feels that perhaps you should still go to Germany, but he loves your company. He's always brighter when you're around. And you would still see some new places. In fact, it might be more exciting for you. And," she ended characteristically, "you're old enough now to think of other people."

"I do try, Granny."

"Yes. Well, I'm glad you're being so sensible about it. And you enjoyed the trip to America so much that no doubt you'll be glad to be on a ship again."

"A ship?"

"Well, yes. There are several possibilities. When we've washed up we'll talk about it more thoroughly. There are some pamphlets and brochures you can look at. There are always cancellations, luckily, so it seems that we have a choice, even at this late date. We could choose a Mediterranean cruise, or one to Holland, Denmark and Norway, or a trip to Madeira, with some time in a hotel there, returning on another ship.''

"Madeira?" repeated Drina, and wondered why that struck a chord. She wasn't even very clear about the position of Madeira. Somewhere off the north-west coast of Africa, surely? And – yes, Yolande had mentioned it in a letter. Something about the Lingeraux Ballet Company going there in the middle of August.

"I went there once, long ago," said Mrs Chester. "It's a delightful island; Portuguese, of course, but British people have been going there for a long time. There are some excellent hotels and the climate is wonderful. I hardly think that we'll consider the Denmark and Norway trip, as the doctor especially mentioned warmth. But the Mediterranean cruise – I don't know. See what you think, only let's finish here first.''

Drina automatically stacked plates in the rack, but while she worked her thoughts began to race.

Not Germany ... Oh, it was a pity, a real disappointment, and Hildegarde would be disappointed, too. But her grandmother was right; she could probably go another time. And there was no doubt that it would be exciting to be on another ship. The memory of those long Atlantic days was still very vivid with Drina, but a ship that was not going to America and Grant ...

"You must write to Hildegarde at once," Mrs Chester was saying. "And we must cancel your air ticket.''

Drina followed her back into the living-room and Mr Chester looked up anxiously over the outspread sheets of *The Times*. He saw at once that she had heard the news and seemed relieved when she said cheerfully:

"Granny's been telling me. She says we've got to choose where we'll go.''

"Don't you mind, then?" he asked. "I thought you might be really upset. I told your grandmother –"

"No, I don't really mind," Drina assured him, though the thought that she would not see Dinkelsbühl still caused her a sharp pang. It was not easy to abandon weeks of dreaming.

"You'll like the sun. You always seem to yearn for it."

"I've never known really hot sun. I went to Italy in April –"

"Well, look." He began to spread out the bright brochures. "This is the Mediterranean one ... Marseilles, La Spezia, Naples, Athens –"

"Greece!" Drina cried wistfully, poring over the pictures.

"Yes, you'd love Greece. But the ship that would take us to Madeira would call at Gibraltar and Casablanca."

Drina wrinkled her nose.

"Casablanca?"

"Don't they teach you geography at school?"

"Well, of course they do. It's in Morocco," she said triumphantly. "Africa! Oh, but I could never see *Africa*!"

"I don't see why on earth not," Mrs Chester said rather tartly.

"Oh, well, it seems unlikely somehow. I imagine it as dark and brooding; so vast."

"Well," Mrs Chester said briskly, having little sympathy with imaginative remarks, "we've really got to make up our minds at once or the cabins will go. We have to telephone this morning."

"A little festival in Funchal," Yolande had written. And Madeira, with its high mountains and cliffs and flowers did sound lovely. If it meant the Lingeraux Company being there at the same time ...

"Let's go to Madeira," said Drina.

"Very well," said Mrs Chester. "I rather hoped

you'd say that. We'll fix it at once. It means leaving Southampton on August 10th."

"So soon?"

"Yes. And you'll need some sun dresses, I suppose.

"And a new swimsuit or something," added Drina, mischievously. She knew her grandmother's views on modern clothing or lack of it.

Mrs Chester looked up sharply.

"What do you mean? Not a bikini or anything like that, because you know I don't –"

"No, no, Granny. Just something suitable for sun-bathing …"

Mrs Chester groaned and her husband laughed.

"If we take her on a cruise ship she must have what other young things have."

"It won't only be the young people," Mrs Chester said grimly. "Women of all ages wear ridiculous garments nowadays. But so long as they wear *something* – oh, stop grinning like that, Drina, and write that letter to Hildegarde."

Later, as Drina started to get Jenny's room ready, her thoughts were whirling. It was some little time before guilt began to take a hold on her. She had chosen Madeira and that was partly because of a glimpse of Africa and partly because of the possibility of ballet there. Maybe it had been dishonest not to explain. Her grandmother often got annoyed by the way she found ballet wherever she went, and this time she had deliberately chosen to go where it might be.

She went out to explain, but her grandfather was on the telephone talking to the shipping office and her grandmother was writing a letter, looking very absorbed.

"Oh, bother!" thought Drina. "*Granny* wanted to go to Madeira. I must leave it now."

She was still feeling rather guilty as she dressed to go and meet Jenny at Paddington the next afternoon. That morning one of her ballet magazines had arrived and it contained a picture of Cécile Barreux, prima ballerina of the Lingeraux Company, with the caption:

"Cécile Barreux is soon to go to Madeira with other members of the Lingeraux Company. They are to dance in Funchal in the Municipal Theatre and the open-air theatre in the public gardens.

"Funchal is to be *en fête* in an attempt to attract visitors in August, which is out of season for the sub-tropical island. As well as ballet dancers they have invited a number of well-known singers and musicians, and part of the South British Shakespeare Company will give scenes from Shakespeare's plays."

It all sounded delightfully exciting, and the cabins were now definitely booked, but Drina shrank from her grandmother's possible displeasure. If she knew that there was actually to be ballet on the island …

Oh, well, it was time to leave. She glanced at herself in the glass and sighed suddenly, aware, as she so often was, that she still looked a child. She was wearing a pink dress and white sandals with almost flat heels, and with her pale face and swinging, straight dark hair looked about thirteen, or not even that. Jenny would be amused and the thought stung. Drina changed the sandals for ones with rather higher heels and applied a fair amount of pink lipstick. Really it was silly not to try and look a little older when she would soon be sixteen.

Mrs Chester was writing more letters and barely looked up when Drina said goodbye.

"Bring Jenny back in a taxi. She's sure to have a fairly heavy case."

In the end Drina was at Paddington early, so she took some money out of her handbag and went to telephone

Rose. Until recently Rose had not been on the phone, but her father had had a rise and Rose's gentle bullying had at last taken effect. She had promised to pay whatever she could towards it, whenever she earned some money.

Rose herself answered.

"Where are you? Paddington? Oh, meeting Jenny. I'm just making a new dress. Mum's helping me, but she's slipped out to the shops. How are the holidays? Still looking forward to Germany?"

"I'm not going."

"Not *going*?" Rose's voice was shrill with horror.

"Not this time. Grandfather has to have a holiday in the sun, and Granny wants me to go, too. So I'm going to Madeira with them."

Rose assimilated this for a moment.

"Oh, poor Hildegarde! She will be sorry. But Madeira sounds more exciting than Germany. You don't know how lucky you are."

"I suppose so."

"You don't sound very cheerful. And it is mean of your grandmother to make you change your plans."

"It isn't that. I shall love the ship, and seeing Gibraltar and Morocco. But Rose, they let me choose, and I chose Madeira because I knew the Lingeraux was going to dance there. I haven't told them –"

"Well, you idiot! What's wrong with that? Ballet for Drina once again!"

"Yes, but now I feel guilty. Granny just hates the way I always find ballet wherever we go. But it's fixed and Granny really has enough to think about –"

"Oh, your troublesome conscience!" Rose groaned. "Why *should* you feel guilty? You're doing it to please them."

"I know, but –"

"Well, forget it. Let her find out when it happens. You can't be too conscientious in this world –"

Drina sighed, but did not argue any more. She arranged to see Rose with Jenny in two days' time, and then walked slowly towards the platform where Jenny's train would arrive.

2
No Escaping Ballet

The train arrived two minutes later and Drina soon saw Jenny in the crowd. She looked taller than ever, and older than ever, too. Her fair hair had been cut very short in a casual, windswept style and she wore a smart cream jacket over a green dress. Her heels were obviously high, and, as she drew nearer, Drina saw that she was wearing a lot of make-up. Once more it was almost impossible to believe that this was the plump little Jenny, who, not so many years ago, had arrived with an eager rush, hair flying.

This new Jenny advanced slowly, lookly oddly self-conscious. Immediately Drina felt self-conscious, too, and found herself babbling:

"Oh, Jenny, how nice to see you! How old you look! Even older than you did last time. And how – how smart."

Jenny grinned then and looked more her old self.

"Bear in mind that, in a few years, it will be no compliment to be told that I look old. Mother made the jacket out of an old coat of hers. Do you like it?"

"It's very nice. But do you go farming like that?"

Jenny grinned again.

"Not on your life. This is the me who is soon going out to work. I can't go to the office in jeans and wellingtons. I'm two people now."

"As long as the other one is still there." The words slipped out.

"It's somewhere," said Jenny brusquely. "Goodness! You *still* look a kid in spite of the lipstick. Didn't Paris do anything for you?"

They were walking towards the taxi queue and Drina was silent for a few moments. Oh, yes, Paris had done a great deal. It had brought her Grant again, and that dreamlike day at Versailles when she loved him so much, but understood why he would not hold her hand. Jenny knew nothing about Grant, where once she would have had all Drina's confidences.

In the taxi Jenny talked, a little feverishly, and Drina continued to be aware of that dreadful stiffness and self-consciousness. Things were no better when they reached the flat, for it was clear – though she did her best to hide it – that Mrs Chester disapproved more than ever of this almost grown up Jenny. And it was not until late that evening, when Jenny was in her pyjamas and curled up at the foot of Drina's bed, that they slipped back into something of their old ease. This had happened on Jenny's last visit, too, but Drina had almost given up hope as the day wore on. However, bathed and wearing a shabby cotton housecoat, Jenny seemed to find that other self and talked more quietly and naturally.

"Well, at least I've got the Grossdale behind me. It's been the worst year of my life, but you know that. And it isn't going to get much better. I loathe and dread the thought of working in an office."

"Will – will you be good at it, then?"

"Oh, good enough. I'm an efficient type. I've *got* to be now. But you haven't had so good a time, either. You look very pale and much thinner than usual."

"It *was* awful," Drina admitted. "How do you think Grandfather looks?"

"Old," Jenny said bluntly, "and very frail. Your granny doesn't look so hot, either. But maybe they'll be better after a holiday. Madeira! Fancy! But then you were born to travel."

"You used to say I was born to dance."

"Perhaps they go together." Soon afterwards Jenny uncoiled herself, yawning, and stood up.

"Good night. I'll be better now. It always takes me a bit of time to get back. I think you're the only one who pulls back my old self. You don't alter. Fame hasn't spoilt you at all. It used to frighten me."

"I'm not famous, Jenny."

Jenny stood looking down at the black-haired figure in the bed.

"It seems like fame to me, you funny, girl. How do you think I feel, reading about you in the newspapers? All the things you've done and you can still say that! You don't know *anything*." And she was gone.

Drina lay thinking for a long time. It was not true that she did not "know anything". She had not worked in the theatre, and had not loved Grant so unexpectedly and deeply, without learning a great deal about the world and herself. But she had kept her values and she had sensed months ago that Jenny was in danger of losing hers. Jenny often said things, and professed to believe things, that came very close to shocking Drina.

But in the days that followed the old Jenny was more in evidence. She left off some of the make-up, changed into shoes with lower heels, and spoke in a much quieter, less aggressive voice. Mrs Chester sighed often, looking at her, but Jenny did not ask for pity and would deeply have resented any sign of it.

Jenny and Drina, and sometimes Rose or Ilonka, walked a good deal, sometimes on Hampstead Heath or across Regent's Park to Primrose Hill, and once they went as far as Epping Forest, when the weather seemed more settled. Jenny had a fondness for the big shops and it was she who helped Drina to buy clothes for the coming holiday, much to Mrs Chester's anxiety. But, mindful of her grandmother, Drina was careful not to choose anything too outrageous and the result was a great many pretty, brightly coloured things that would be ideal on the ship and in Madeira.

"You're so lucky!" said Jenny often and did not let pride stand in the way when Mr Chester gave her some money and told her to buy something pretty for herself.

"I oughtn't to take it, I suppose," she said later. "But he has known me for a long time – he's almost a kind of relation."

When they were alone Jenny talked a good deal of Robert Hogden and once said:

"Sometimes I think I'm in love with him. But you wouldn't know about that." And Drina did not enlighten her, merely said:

"Oh, Jenny, you always *said* you'd marry a farmer. And it would be such a perfect solution."

Jenny gave her an odd look.

"So it would."

"But you couldn't marry for years and years."

"Have you forgotten that I'm sixteen? Legally –"

"Oh, yes, but you wouldn't –"

"Wait and see," said Jenny and changed the subject abruptly.

So the days passed pleasantly and Drina was lulled by the presence almost of the old Jenny, and the thought of the coming holiday in the sun. She began to feel less tired and life seemed safer and happier again. It was a shock when Jenny said slowly on their last evening, when they were alone in Drina's room:

"Look, Drina, I've got a feeling – I think something's brewing."

"*Brewing*?" asked Drina, in an instant panic. "Trouble? What *do* you mean?"

"I don't quite know. I just sense something and it seems only fair to warn you, if you haven't sniffed it out for yourself. I know what your granny is: she never tells you things. Haven't you felt it yourself? An atmosphere?"

"Not really," Drina faltered. "We've been out such a lot, and – and I've been thinking about Morocco and Madeira. Buying maps, reading it up – you *know*."

"Well, I may be wrong. Don't get in a panic. But it does seem to me there's something. So many rather mysterious telephone calls, and you remarked yourself that there'd been rather a number of strangers here. You remember that man and woman who were just leaving when we got back from Epping Forest? Your grandmother was very cagey about them. And several times she and your grandfather have stopped talking abruptly when we came into the room."

"Y – yes, now you mention it – but, Jenny, what could it be? There's only one thing. Granny did say something about moving away from the river. But I thought she'd forgotten. She really ought to tell me things now I'm older."

"She won't alter. It's her way. It's not as though she's your mother; she's two generations away from you. Look how they took you out of Willerbury and away from the Selswick."

"I was only eleven then." But the memory was still sharp and painful. "Anyway, they wouldn't move far away from the Dominick. Only up to St John's Wood or Primrose Hill or somewhere like that. Higher and less foggy. Oh, *Jenny*!"

"I wish I'd said nothing," said Jenny morosely. "But I've a nose for trouble these days. Forget it."

And Drina did almost forget it, as there was so little time for thought. Once Jenny had gone there was an orgy of packing and label-writing, and on August 9th they went down to Southampton. Mrs Chester hated early starts and preferred a night in a hotel to catching an early boat train from Waterloo.

It was strange to be in Southampton again and it brought back very forcibly that other evening eleven months before when they had been on the point of sailing to New York on the *Queen of the Atlantic*. The *Queen of the Atlantic* ... perhaps she would be in at that very moment.

Drina slipped away and walked down the High Street towards the docks. It was a bright, almost hot afternoon and the water was blue and sparkling. Once she reached the farthest corner her heart lurched, for there was the familiar liner rearing up above other, far smaller ships. Standing there, she wished passionately that she was returning to America and not going south into the sun.

But the next morning genuine excitement had her in its grip and she was so restless to be on board the *Balmoral* that Mrs Chester was quite irritable.

"We'll only have to wait if we go early, Drina. The embarkation notice says between ten and ten-thirty and she doesn't sail until noon."

But at last they were speeding towards the docks and the *Balmoral* turned out to be a large white ship with yellow funnels. Not nearly so big as the *Queen of the Atlantic*, of course, but large enough. Their cabins were outside ones on A Deck, and Drina drew a deep breath of satisfaction when she was alone in hers, examining the wardrobe, the dressing-table and all the fittings.

"The luggage will be along soon," said Mrs Chester, looking in. "Yes, it's very nice; large for a single cabin. What a lucky girl you are."

Drina felt guilty as she knelt to unlock her cases. Jenny would have welcomed the smallest and darkest cabin on any ship.

Drina was up on the Boat Deck when the ship sailed, and her heart leaped when the sirens gave a shrill blast. She always found the sailing of a great ship very moving and she was glad that she was alone, leaning on the rail, feeling the heat of the sun. For it was a really lovely morning at last and the air was almost windless as they slipped away down Southampton Water towards the Isle of Wight, the Needles and the Channel.

Unpacking could wait until later and she began eagerly to explore the ship, padding lightly in her sandals through the public rooms – the library, the huge lounge, the different bars, the dance floor. The sight of the hard floor and clear stretch there tempted her and she did a few ballet steps before a grinning steward made her find the stairs again and come out on one of the open promenade decks.

The dining-room stewards were friendly and the service was good. Mrs Chester began to relax and Mr Chester said happily:

"I think we'll have a very pleasant trip. I shall sit in a sheltered part of the deck after lunch. I don't suppose the pool is open yet, Drina, but you won't be bored?"

"Oh, no, Grandfather," said Drina hastily. Boredom was a thing that rarely troubled her.

After the meal, and coffee in the lounge, she helped her grandmother to unpack, then unpacked her own things and wandered back to the deck. Her grandmother was now resting in the big double cabin, but she found her grandfather without difficulty in a sheltered corner aft. He was studying the passenger list and he looked up, smiling, when she dropped down beside him.

"Have you looked at the passenger list?"

"Oh, no. I've got one, but there hasn't been time."

"There are two names that you'll know. Maybe others." Drina followed the line of his pointing finger, her hair swinging forward.

"Madame Lingeraux! Oh, it – it never occurred to me that she'd – that they'd be on *this* ship!"

"And Cécile Barreux. Isn't she their prima ballerina? But what do you mean? Did you expect Madame Lingeraux to be on *some* ship, then?"

Drina gulped and all her doubts rushed back.

"Grandfather, there's a sort of Festival in Funchal; just a little one. The Lingeraux is going to Madeira for that. But I suppose I thought that they might fly."

He looked shrewdly at her downbent face. "I thought you'd be delighted. Why are you looking like that, Drina?"

Then it all came out with a rush.

"Yolande mentioned it before – before you ever asked me to choose. It was partly why I *did* choose Madeira. Then I – I felt mean, and guilty, because I know how Granny feels. You know, ballet *everywhere*. Only Rose laughed at me, and the cabins were booked, and so –"

He took her hand gently. He was smiling.

"Then *I'm* guilty, too. I knew about that Festival, but I whipped the brochure about it out of your grandmother's sight. If you *hadn't* chosen Madeira, I'd have given you a hint."

"Oh, Grandfather! That was – was a bit wicked of you. But really great. Only what will she say?"

"She'll get over it," he said comfortably. "I thought it would give you an extra interest. I suppose you'll meet them sooner or later, even amongst several hundred passengers. Do you know what Madame looks like?"

"Small, fat, elderly, terribly ugly, with a slight moustache," said Drina, grinning. "Lots of personality, I should think. Not a bit like Miss Volonaise, of course, who is beautiful. I've seen Madame Lingeraux once or twice. She's been to the Dominick matinées. The shows the students, give, you know."

"Hoping to nab talent?"

"I don't know. Maybe just out of interest. They do all seem to keep in touch. I shall know her if I see her." Drina took the passenger list and picked out other names that seemed familiar. "Carol Collingwood. I think she's the one Yolande used to know. She's the youngest member of the Company. They must all be here. Oh, it is fun, isn't it? Especially as you think I needn't feel guilty."

"Guilty, rubbish!" he said fondly. "You feel guilty about far too many things, but it's nice of you. Run away and see if you can find any of them."

But she did not see Madame Lingeraux or anyone who looked like a ballet dancer. The ship was large, and, as her grandfather had said, there were several hundred passengers. But there were a number of young people and she spent most of the afternoon playing deck tennis.

At dinner Mrs Chester looked at her rather grimly.

"Ballet on board, I hear, *and* in Madeira. Really, there's no escaping it."

"Oh, Granny, I'm sorry if you mind," Drina said, contritely. "But I've certainly escaped it so far. I haven't seen a soul who looks like a dancer."

Mrs Chester grunted.

"I've seen Madame."

"You *haven't*? Where? I didn't know you knew her!"

Her grandmother gave her an almost mischievous smile.

"In the ladies' room on A Deck, if you must know. I used to know her, but she's certainly aged. What an ugly woman, yet she still moves like a dancer in spite of all that extra weight. You never will give me credit for knowing people in the ballet world. Betsy knew her, though the Lingeraux wasn't much in those days. Not much now, except for short experimental things. They're not a large enough company to give first-class performances of the big classical ballets."

"It's true, of course, but they do some interesting new things. Maybe I'll see them after dinner."

"I doubt it, the first night. Everyone will be tired, and you're to go to bed early. I don't believe you slept well last night."

Drina annoyed herself by giving, at that very moment, a suppressed yawn, and Mrs Chester laughed.

"Go up on deck for a few minutes when you've had your coffee, and then off to bed."

It was nearly sunset when Drina climbed to the Boat Deck. The water was calm and dark blue and there was not much wind, in spite of the ship's speed. She thought with wonder that by early Saturday morning they would reach Gibraltar. It would be very odd to see the famous Rock, and stranger still to set foot in Morocco. She felt very happy suddenly; happy and excited. With England now behind them, her problems seemed to have fallen behind, too, and she no longer even regretted Germany. But she did spare one thought, looking westwards, to New York far away across the ocean, rising in towers of concrete and glass and steel into the sky. Grant would be nowhere near going to bed, as New York was five hours behind in time, but she thought, as she nearly always did, "Good

night, Grant!" and then went two decks down to her
cabin.

Lulled by the distant swish of water and the steady
movement of the ship, she was asleep almost at once.

Having gone to bed early Drina was awake early and
long before the gong had sounded for first breakfast
(they were second sitting, in any case) she was restless.
The pool would probably have been filled by now and
she went out to make sure. It was only a few steps
away, on the same deck, in the open air, and she heard
splashes and cheerful shouts before she saw it properly.
That was all right, then, and it seemed another warm
morning, with bright sunshine.

She returned to her cabin and put on her red
swimsuit, but was checked on her second trip towards
the pool by the sound of music from up above. Almost
outside her cabin, stairs rose to the next deck and the
open door of the dance floor, and the piano music came
clearly, with a familiar beat that was unmistakable.
Drina gasped and bolted up the stairs, her hair
bouncing on her shoulders.

The sight that met her eyes was one not usually seen
on a cruise ship. About thirty men and girls wearing
practice costume were taking part in a vigorous centre
practice, the class conducted by a dumpy, elderly
woman with a penetrating voice. Around the sides of
the dance floor, obviously fascinated, stood a few early
risers amongst the passengers, but the dancers were
clearly oblivious of them. Drina's bare feet positively
itched to join in as she stood there, and just then
Madame Lingeraux called "Rest!" and, apparently
moved by some instinct, turned round.

Her sharp, dark eyes met Drina's and after a moment
she said:

"Drina Adams? Good morning, my dear. Do you want to join in?"

Drina positively gaped. How on *earth* did Madame Lingeraux know her?

"Don't tell me you've come without ballet shoes?"

"Oh, no. No, of course not. I always bring them. Yes, Madame, I'd – I'd love to join the class."

"Then hurry up," said Madame imperiously.

Drina bolted back to her cabin and threw shoes wildly out of the wardrobe until she found a pair of ballet slippers. Tying them carefully she heard the music start again, but it was only a very short time before she was on the dance floor again and finding a place near the back of the class. Near the front was Cécile Barreux and next to Drina was a dark-haired boy, who looked astonished by her sudden presence.

When the class was over he reached for a towel on the platform behind him and said:

"Where did you come from? I saw Madame speak to you. You're very advanced for a kid of your age."

Drina, towelless, for she had left it in her cabin, glared at him, noting that he was very good-looking and not so old himself. Probably not more than seventeen or eighteen.

"I'll have you know that I'll soon be sixteen."

"Well, now!" he said, amused. "I'm sorry."

"And I don't know *how* Madame knew me. I'm Drina Adams –"

"*Drina Adams!*" he repeated. "Not the Drina Adams who was in *Diary of a Dancer* for a while? And danced Little Clara –?"

"Yes."

"I *thought* you looked familiar. I'm sorry I insulted you."

"It's nothing new," said Drina, good-tempered again. "People always think I'm a kid." She never grew used to being recognised and there was no doubt that it was pleasing. "It seems like fame to me," Jenny had said.

"I'm Jasper Blane," he said. "I've been in the Company for six months. Here's Madame!"

Madame Lingeraux advanced with that quick, easy walk that was the heritage of her long-ago dancing days. She was, as Drina had said, a remarkably ugly woman, but one did not remember that for long.

Jasper melted away as Drina faced Madame.

"It – it was so nice of you to let me –"

"Well, it's common sense, isn't it? You'll want to practise. Not ideal, of course. We did our *barre* work as best we could on the open stretch of deck, where at least the hand-rail is well-placed. Every morning at seven-thirty. Before too many people are about."

"But – but you don't *know* me, Madame!"

Madame Lingeraux cackled. Or it was very close to being a cackle.

"Bless me, child, I know you well enough. And your grandmother told me you were on board. I must say it was a shock. I didn't realise that you were the Chesters' grandchild – Ivory's daughter."

Drina went very white; this had not occurred to her.

"Oh, please, Madame, don't! Have you mentioned it to anyone?"

Madame Lir.geraux looked at her shrewdly.

"No, I haven't. Mrs Chester told me you were cagey about it. Do you mean to say that you've deliberately kept it dark, about being Ivory's daughter?"

"Of course I have. I wanted to succeed on my own, without the – the impetus of her name. But Mr Dominick and Miss Volonaise found out."

"I bet they were thrilled," said Madame, in her downright way. "Ivory's daughter! What School could want more?"

"I – I don't think they feel like that. I'm very unimportant at the Dominick."

Once more the cackle rang out, but Madame's voice was comfortingly low.

"You're very modest, and of course it is too early to tell if you've inherited the whole of her talent. I've seen you dance and act and read your notices. That was a good little ballet you choreographed last Christmas."

"*Twentieth Century Serenade*? Oh, thank you! But I wasn't in it. I was too busy rehearsing for the Christmas play at Francaster."

"Marianne Volonaise told me you danced in it in New York. Well, look! You'll get cold. Don't go diving into the pool when you're so hot. We haven't reached a sub-tropical climate yet."

Drina escaped and was almost at her cabin door when a voice called her breathlessly. Drina turned round. A young girl, her straight fair hair tied back with a ribbon, was hurrying after her.

"You're Drina Adams? I'm Carol Collingwood. Yolande's written about you from New York. I used to live next door to her."

"Yes, I know. I'd heard. How do you do?"

"Very well, thank you, and delighted to be going to Madeira. Are you going to join us?"

"Well, Madame asked me to join the classes."

"Of course. Very sensible. Are you going to stay in Madeira."

"Yes."

"Good. How's the Dominick?"

"Still there, for the time being," said Drina sadly.

"Yes, we heard it's going. Moving, rather. I must say

we'd hate to lose our old building in Bloomsbury Square. Well, I'll see you later. Great to have met you."

Drina went thoughtfully to have a hot salt bath, since it did seem unwise to swim just then. She was thoroughly content and the immediate future looked rosy. Ballet on board the *Balmoral*!

"I always am lucky," she said to herself, as the green water reached warmly to her shoulders.

3

Sunshine and
Flowers

Mrs Chester was gloomy but resigned when she heard about the early morning events.

"I *knew* it! Why couldn't Madame let well alone? They're all older and more experienced. Naturally."

"Well, they are, Granny. I never expected to take part in a class with a prima ballerina. But I can keep up, just about, and Madame can't bite *my* head off."

"Did she bite any?"

"One or two. She's a martinet. Carol Collingwood seems really nice, and she can't be more than seventeen. Barely that. And Jasper Blane seems nice, too. He thought I was a *child* at first."

Mr Chester laughed at her disgusted tone, but Mrs Chester frowned.

"So you are. Fifteen was a child in my day."

"It isn't in mine," said Drina, grinning.

Her grandmother eyed her warily, and suddenly, as so often happened nowadays, she wished passionately that her daughter Betsy had lived to bring up her own child. She often found herself out of her depth with Drina now, and had, in fact, been puzzled and vaguely uneasy since the time on the *Queen of the Atlantic*. Instinct told her that Drina had altered abruptly then, but reason had not given her the answer. It had never once occurred to her that falling in love had caused the change. She merely assumed vaguely that adolescence was an awkward time.

"I don't understand her any more," she said to her husband, when Drina had raced off to play deck tennis.

"Did you ever?" he asked mildly and she flushed right up to her silvery hair.

"My dear James! I've looked after her since she was quite a small baby."

"I know," he said, "but there was always a side that beat you. You used to call it the Italian side. Drina's all right; a thousand times better than many girls. She has sense."

"I wouldn't call it sense. So much emotionalism –"

"That's her artistic temperament, but she has got a core of hard sense. You can safely leave her to grow up her own way."

"You always spoilt her."

"And you were always a little hard on her," he said gently.

Mrs Chester sighed in an exasperated way, but her glance softened as she looked at his face.

"I never meant to be. She needs a strong hand in my opinion. All young people do. Look at the way they go on nowadays –"

"Drina doesn't 'go on'. She works hard and suffers a good deal because she's sensitive."

Mrs Chester argued no more just then. They had already argued much during the last few weeks and her mind was made up.

Meanwhile Drina had no idea that she was being discussed. She had already allowed herself to sink into that strange kind of limbo that seemed an integral part of life at sea. It was unreal and yet, in contradiction, she had a heightened feeling of being alive.

Throughout that long sunny day she was really happy. It seemed now peculiar that she had seen no ballet dancers the previous afternoon and evening. They seemed all over the ship and even Cécile Barreux, sitting in a deckchair wearing glamorous beach clothes, called her over.

"Come and talk to me for a while. Madame says you're the Drina Adams who's been in several West End plays and who danced Little Clara at the Edinburgh Festival. In Paris, too, wasn't it?"

"Yes." Drina sat down shyly.

"You'll know Catherine Colby?"

"Well, I do. Yes. But she is – was – very important." Catherine Colby, until her retirement, had been prima ballerina of the Dominick Company, but, as it happened, Drina had got to know her quite well. For one thing Catherine Colby, her husband, Peter Bernoise, and their small daughter Penelope had been on the *Queen of the Atlantic* during that momentous trip to America.

They gossiped cheerfully for some time, and Carol, joining Drina soon afterwards, seemed impressed.

"Very friendly, wasn't she? We all think her rather remote, though she can be very kind. She's engaged to Michael Mann."

Drina's eyes at once went to a sun-tanned figure just about to plunge into the pool.

"Your principal male dancer? He's – he's very good-looking."

"Oh, he's all right. We all like him. Now come and sit in the sun and tell me about Yolande in New York."

But it was Jasper Blane who, as the day wore on, came over to Drina several times and eventually stayed by her side, urging her to play table tennis, then to have another swim. Sitting on towels afterwards, they exchanged life histories and Drina was interested to learn that Jasper, too, had had a struggle to become a dancer. He came from a London family, in which there was a dash of Polish blood on his mother's side. She was artistic and had been successful in her early years with her painting, but his father was a University lecturer and had wanted his only son to be a teacher.

"It was grim. Even when I was a kid I knew I wanted to dance and Dad kept on about studying. Eventually I won and went to the Lingeraux. He's never really got over it. He thinks that all dancers are sissy."

By now Jasper was stretched out full-length, already browning in the sun and sea wind, and Drina eyed his athletic body thoughtfully.

"He can't possibly think *you* sissy!"

"Psychologically. I'm not, of course. I'm as tough as can be. But it's even sissy to be going to dance in Madeira when I ought to be on the point of going to Oxford."

"Perhaps you'd never have got there."

"More than likely. I wasn't brilliant. Oh, well, here we are – and very pleasant it is." And he smiled up at Drina.

That evening Drina put on the emerald green dress that she had bought at the famous New York store, Saks, Fifth Avenue. There was to be a dance that night, starting at nine-thirty, and over coffee in the lounge her grandmother said:

"You were up early and have had a long day. I think you had better go to bed. You're really too young –"

"Oh, Granny!" Drina cried rebelliously. "I'm not a bit tired and I *wish* you wouldn't keep on saying that I'm too young for things."

"Well, for half an hour, then. But if you're getting up

for that ballet class at seven-thirty –"

"I don't need more than eight hours sleep," said Drina and just then found Jasper at her elbow.

She introduced him to her grandparents, thinking that he looked extremely different, but just as good-looking, in more formal clothes. Mrs Chester was pleasant but reserved, and the two young people soon hurried away. Couples were already dancing and the ship's band blared out. Drina shuddered at the saxophone, which was an instrument that – even at its very best – never appealed to her, but it was fun to be dancing, part of that happy crowd. Later one or two of the other young men in the Lingeraux Company asked her to dance and it was nearly eleven o'clock when she saw her grandmother standing by one of the doors.

Drina whirled across the floor, her full green skirts flying out.

"Granny, I'm sorry, but I was having such fun! I'll go to bed now."

"You certainly don't look tired, and I must say that the Bay of Biscay has behaved wonderfully well. Good night, Drina."

Drina kissed her and shot down the stairs to her cabin. It had been a wonderful day.

The next day the weather was soft and really warm, the sea was almost waveless, and they steamed past the high red cliffs of Portugal. Seeing the occasional little villages of white houses, and sometimes a small, high church, Drina was thrilled. It seemed, now, that all the worry of the summer term had been a bad dream and when she looked at her face in the glass it was smooth and brown, the slight shadows gone from beneath her eyes. And more was to come, far more. Gibraltar in the morning and seven hours ashore.

Mrs Chester said that she and Mr Chester would not be going ashore. Drina was going with Jasper and Carol and some of the others.

"It's sure to be very hot. You must buy one of those big straw hats they have in the ship's shop," Mrs Chester said.

That evening, Drina and Jasper walked slowly round the Boat Deck under the brilliant summer stars. It was very warm and Drina was happy, but a little nostalgic. She liked Jasper, and had not missed the fact that he was beginning to be attracted to her, but if *only* he were Grant! Grant who had been on that other ship speeding westwards across the Atlantic. Grant who had stood with her on top of the RCA Building on that last night in America, with the lights of New York making an unforgettable pattern below. The thought that she would not see him again for about a year gripped her suddenly and painfully and Jasper touched her arm.

"What's the matter?"

"Nothing: it's getting late, you know. Granny will be cross. I think I'd better go now."

"No, don't. It's such a lovely night. You look – rather like a green elf." The words came with some difficulty, as though he were not used to paying compliments.

"A changeling. I was once, in a ballet," Drina countered lightly, and firmly led the way to the nearest steps. Strangely, perhaps, she felt older than he, and it was no use letting him get *too* attracted.

She took a last look at the star-lit sea from the door that led on to the deck near her cabin and thought suddenly of Jenny.

"You don't know *anything*!"

"But I do," she thought, "and I'd hate Jasper to be

hurt. I expect it's only being at sea, and the stars and everything, though. It's such a romantic setting."

In the morning the coast of Spain and many white houses showed through a blue mist, and there was the vast Rock, rearing up: But the blue haze lay thickly on its long ridge and dimmed the climbing streets and little squares. Other ships lay at anchor on the still water. It was strange to see Gibraltar in reality, as though it had stepped straight out of a geography book.

It was stranger still to go ashore in the crowded tender, feeling the bite of the sun even at a comparatively early hour, and to step ashore on a hot jetty. Most of the notices were in English and advertisements were for familiar things, but the overall impression was very foreign. Drina and her friends avoided a number of eager taxi drivers and set off briskly under a stone gateway into the crowded shopping thoroughfare, Main Street. This was lined with shops selling a variety of goods, some of them little more than bazaars, and the place was jammed with other visitors.

They wandered up a steep side street, finding at once a different atmosphere. Here were sun-drenched white buildings, palm trees, cobbled squares and playing children. And now magic, too, was there for Drina, in the knowledge that she was actually in Gibraltar, seeing a new place.

She wandered slowly along, drinking it all in, her face intent under the big red and white straw hat. Presently they found themselves back in Main Street, where, by way of a tiny courtyard with a fountain, they ended up in the cool near-dark of the Catholic Cathedral.

They had planned to go on to the Alameda Gardens, so they left the main part of the town by way of a second, very impressive stone gateway in high walls, and were again in possession of sunlight and quietness. On one side of the road was a tiny, shady cemetery – the Trafalgar Cemetery, Drina's map told her – and on the other side were some very small gardens, deep down and surrounded by high stone walls. The others flung themselves down under a shady tree, but Drina ran down the slope and breathed in the sweet smell of flowers and hedges of rosemary. Here was enchantment indeed, for the flowers were exotic ones … pink and white oleanders, trails of purple bougainvillaea, and the blazing scarlet of hibiscus. They were all past their best, now that it was August, but lovely for all that.

She drifted round the little paths, sniffing the scented air often, then climbed the slope again and went on along a blazing hot road towards the much bigger Alameda Gardens. These she seemed, amazingly, to have almost to herself, and the colours of the flowers and flowering shrubs took her breath right away. It was something that she had never known before, except briefly and not so overpoweringly in Italy, and something that she had always craved.

Happiness had the inevitable result; she flung down her sunhat and the bag that held the fruit, biscuits and chocolate she had brought for a picnic lunch, and began to dance, as she had once danced in the gardens on Isola Bella. Believing herself quite alone, she tucked a hibiscus flower into her hair and, with another in her hand, pirouetted lightly along the sun-dappled path.

But Igor had seen her on Isola Bella, and now, to her chagrin and dismay, Jasper was there. He had come quite suddenly round a corner and was staring at her as though she were indeed an elfin creature.

Drina laughed as casually as she could and threw the red flowers away.

"It takes me that way sometimes. Isn't it lovely, Jasper? The sun and the flowers –"

Jasper still didn't speak and she went on:

"Where are the others?"

"Somewhere about," said Jasper vaguely, and then: "Oh, Drina, you looked fantastic! Do dance again."

But the spell was broken and she was self-conscious and a little cross. It was a relief when Carol and the others appeared and someone suggested getting a bus to the lighthouse on Europa Point.

After the point, they climbed some way up the Rock to see the famous monkeys and later went to St Michael's Cave, with its wonderful stalagmites and stalactites.

In the middle of the afternoon, when they made their way slowly back, towards the jetty, Main Street was shadeless and silent in the depth of the siesta and the blaze of the white buildings near the waterfront was almost dazzling.

It was sad to go away so soon, but there would be other flowers and other sunshine … *Africa*! It was so near, though they had not seen it as they stood on Europa Point because of the haze.

But by five o'clock, when the ship sailed, every detail of the Rock was clear, and schools of porpoise played in the clear, brilliant water. Soon the high blue mountains of North Africa were there, rearing up in the soft and glimmering evening, and they passed close to Tangier, seeing the white buildings climbing the hills.

Drina stood alone in a hidden corner of the Boat Deck, staring, lost in the magic and the unbelievable beauty. To see Africa looking so blue and mystical was not what she had imagined, for it was the Dark Continent, surely, and should have looked brooding and somehow unreachable.

She could scarcely bring herself to go below to change for dinner, and when she did move she met Madame Lingeraux in the passage on A Deck. Shreds of her dreaminess still lingered and at first she hardly knew what Madame was saying.

"I've been talking to your grandparents, child. Why, what's the matter? Have you had too much sun?"

"No – o. I never could have. I – I've been looking at Africa."

Madame accepted this remark as perfectly natural, where Mrs Chester would have been irritated and even disquieted.

"So have I. Not for the first time, but on such an evening ... But come to earth, child. How would you like to dance with us in Madeira?"

Drina did, at once, come fully to earth. She gaped.

"With your Company? Oh, but – I'd *love* to, of course, but – but I don't belong and – and Granny would never agree. She'd say I must have a rest. Not that I need one now."

The familiar cackle rang out.

"She did say just that, but I talked her round. I knew you'd enjoy it and it seems a good idea. We're not at full strength, and, though we've got a fairly packed programme, we could do with one extra item, especially for the little open-air theatre, where we'll dance without scenery. You'll know that we're giving several of the best known *pas de deux* and *pas de quatre*, and scenes from *Swan Lake* and *Casse Noisette*. I thought you might like to dance in the Waltz of the Flowers – we'll be rehearsing in Funchal – and then I wondered ... What about that little ballet of yours, *Twentieth Century Serenade*?"

Drina jumped.

"Oh, Madame, it's months since I even thought about

it. And – and it needs two; two girls. It's not a proper *pas de deux*. And then the others mightn't like it."

Madame looked grim.

"Are you telling me what my Company will or will not like?"

"Oh, no. Y – yes. I didn't mean –"

"I've asked them, as a matter of fact, and they're perfectly willing. I thought you could teach it to Carol. It will be a first little solo role for her and she's a promising dancer. If you wouldn't mind lending us your ballet?"

"No, I shouldn't, of course. I – I should be terribly honoured."

Madame smiled at the stumbling words.

"I shall send a radio message to Mr Dominick, though I don't suppose he'll mind lending me a dancer. But we'd better be courteous. All right?"

"Oh, *yes*, Madame. If Granny –"

"It was your grandfather, really," she said, already turning on her heel. "He said you must be allowed to dance, if you wish."

"Oh!"

"He's quiet, but he gets his way."

"Not very often," said Drina faintly, but the dumpy figure had gone, with remarkable speed, up the stairs.

Drina, somewhat breathless, reached her cabin and dropped her clothes in a heap on the floor. What a day! Sunshine and flowers … a soft and windless evening, with a delicious heat that was not going to die with the coming of the rapid southern dusk … a chance to dance in Madeira.

Life, as she had thought often before, was very satisfying and exciting.

4

Funchal "En Fête"

There was no ballet class the next morning, but most of the dancers were up even earlier than usual for a first glimpse of Casablanca. Well before seven o'clock there it was, its skyscrapers looming up in the faint hot mist beyond the great harbour. The *Balmoral* swept slowly past a long breakwater and then slid more and more slowly towards the quays.

"It does seem – kind of unlikely," said Drina to Jasper, who was by her side on deck, wearing shorts.

"Africa?" he asked, and she nodded. "It looks very new."

"I think it is mostly pretty modern," said Drina, who always read places up beforehand. "Very French, of course, in lots of ways. But there are the old Arab quarters."

"Are you coming out with us today?" Jasper asked. "We're going to see the city this morning. Carol was moaning because it's Sunday and most of the shops will be shut. Then this afternoon –"

"Grandfather said something about going ashore this morning. We're going to take a taxi round the city and then go to some hotel out at Anfa they've been told about."

Jasper's face fell.

"Oh, but you'd have more fun with us!"

"I know. But I *am* with them and I haven't really seen much of them."

"But that's only this morning. Come with us this afternoon. We're all going to hire taxis and go to Mohammedia* to bathe. You couldn't miss that: bathing from an African beach."

Mohammedia was, as Drina knew, about twenty-five miles along the coast, and she was sorely tempted.

"I'll ask. I'd love to, of course."

Breakfast was earlier than usual and she arrived at the table looking so tanned and happy that Mrs Chester was amazed. There was air-conditioning in the dining-room, but the heat outside had already seemed to her intense.

"Good gracious, Drina! How well you look! Don't you mind the heat?"

"I adore it with every fibre of my being," said Drina, so passionately that her grandmother frowned and then laughed.

"Extravagant, as usual! It certainly seems to suit you. I'll take the trip we planned this morning, but this afternoon we'll both stay on board and rest."

"Oh, then, please, Granny, may I go to Mohammedia with the others to bathe? I don't suppose it will cost so very much if we all share taxis and I should like to. I wish I could go to Rabat and see the Royal Palace –"

"That's too far," said Mrs Chester instantly. "Think if you missed the ship. Well, I don't know. What do you think, James?"

"Of course she must go to Mohammedia," Mr Chester said promptly. "It may be years before she's ever in Morocco again."

*Sometimes Fedala.

The heat seemed to shimmer and dance round them as they went down the gangway about nine o'clock, and Drina wore a white sun-dress and her red and white sunhat. The taxis were beautiful cars and the driver they selected spoke good English. They drove away into the modern city, past a row of bazaars, and were soon in wide boulevards with brilliant flower-beds. Drina craned her head out of the open window. The buildings were high and white and the shops looked splendid. All the notices were in French.

The Palais de Justice was in a great square and blood-red flags vied with blood-red flowers. There were palm trees and flowering shrubs all along the boulevards, and once a great white gateway under which Arabs sat lazily in the shade.

Then they came to the Place de la Mosquée, where a great Mosque reared its high tower above the low Arab quarters, with their arches and tiny windows. The driver said that if they would like it he would walk with them through the Arab quarters. Mrs Chester looked as though she would refuse, but Drina was so eager that her grandfather was already out of the car.

Followed by a few beautiful Arab children, they walked through the shadowy courtyards and under stone arcades. In the courtyards old men sat playing a kind of chess game and others were polishing brass. The Chesters bought some brass ash-trays and a small brass jug and Drina two leather purses to take home as presents.

Afterwards they drove past the vast white Cathedral along avenues that grew more and more flowery and came to the hotel at Anfa, a suburb of Casablanca. Here sweet scents hung in the hot air, but the hotel itself was wonderfully cool, with a pool and fountain in the entrance hall. They went up in a lift to a high bar and restaurant, where they sat on an open terrace. Mr and Mrs Chester had coffee and Drina an iced fruit drink. But she soon wandered away round the roof, enchanted by the wide views of Casablanca and the blue ocean. Looking down on one side she saw a brilliant emerald green swimming-pool, surrounded by palm trees and flowers, and when she returned to her grandparents she said:

"Oh, isn't it dreamlike! Fancy spending a winter here, away from cold and rain and fog!"

To her great surprise they both looked immensely startled, and Mrs Chester said in a strange voice:

"What about the Dominick?"

The Dominick seemed far away on this high Moroccan roof-top, and so, for the matter of that, did an English winter, Drina said slowly:

"Of course I couldn't. You know that."

Mrs Chester rose abruptly and said that the taxi driver would be tired of waiting. They drove back to the ship in unusual silence and Drina felt very worried, for she could not understand their strange behaviour. There was no *question*, surely, of her spending a winter out of England?

But by early afternoon she had quite forgotten the odd little incident, for almost the whole of the Lingeraux party, even Madame, piled into taxis and drove away westwards. The road was fairly close to the sea, but the land rose a little, mostly hiding it. This was not real desert, more of a kind of wasteland of beaten earth, bone-dry in the sun, with here and there patches of maize, but it was alien enough to be fascinating, and when she saw her first camels Drina cried out in amazement.

"How funny they look out of a zoo!"

Madame, it seemed, knew an hotel at Mohammedia

and had arranged for them to use its private beach. The hotel was enormous, absolutely modern and in grounds so beautiful and brilliant that everything was more dreamlike than ever. Leaving Madame sitting under a coloured umbrella in the garden, they all streamed down to the beach, dazzled by the brightness of flowers and sun umbrellas and water.

And Drina thought, as her toes ploughed through sand that was so hot as to be almost unbearable:

"I am in Africa ... Morocco. This is me, Drina Adams, in Africa, and I may never, never be here again in my whole life." This was a trick that she often played and it resulted, always, in a feeling of heightened awareness. Now she felt utterly and sharply alive and knew that the moment would last for ever, along with those other memorable moments of her life.

They splashed and raced and shouted to each other; that is, the younger ones did. Cécile Barreux, Michael Mann and the older and more important members of the Company were much more subdued.

"Look at those *children!*" said Michael Mann indulgently.

"Drina's the only child here!" Carol retorted blithely.

But Drina didn't care. For once she was not prepared to argue about age.

When they wandered back, all rather sandy and salty and very thirsty, Madame had ordered tea for everyone and they all sat round her, their brown bodies relaxed. Quite a number of visitors stared at them and said to each other – in a variety of languages – that there was the English ballet company and how good-looking they all were.

"We danced in Bergen and it rained *all* the time," said Carol. "We loved Norway, but it would have been nice to see it in sunshine. We went up in the funicular and *froze*."

"I will arrange," said Madame, grinning, "that you dance only in hot countries in future. But you know you don't like it so well when it comes to working."

"We like it *now*, Madame. It's purest heaven!"

Drina wandered away while the others were still talking, sniffing the sweet fragrance of pine trees and hot grass. But she was not alone for long, for Jasper followed her.

"I haven't seen you alone all day, Drina."

"No," agreed Drina, standing in the shade of a tree and gazing back at the white blaze of the hotel. He, however, was staring at her, his face tense.

"Drina, I think I'm in love with you. You're so beautiful –"

"I always think I'm rather plain," she said. It was not the way to take a compliment, as she was well aware, but it was the truth and Jasper made her feel uneasy when he looked like that, so eager. He had said that he was tough, and so he was, in many ways, but she sensed that she alone had the power to hurt him just now. Better, if possible, to keep their relationship on the sensible level of friendship.

"Plain!" he said. "I've been haunted by the way you danced yesterday in the Alameda Gardens. Drina –" And, before she could stop him, he had kissed her. It was only on her cheek, and because she moved, his lips ended up on her ear.

"I don't think you'd better do that," said Drina. She didn't want him to kiss her, which was a pity in such a lovely place.

"But perhaps we – we can see each other in London. Can't we?" he insisted, as she remained silent.

"I – I suppose so. But I work hard; I'm always busy. And Granny –"

"Oh, I know she guards you," he said ruefully.

"I don't really blame her. Have you ever been in love?"

"It's a question you shouldn't ask," she said lightly and saw that he was even hurt by that.

"Perhaps not. But I thought that girls talked about it all the time. Even the kids in the Lingeraux School –"

"And the kids in the Dominick," she said cheerfully. "Oh, Jasper, don't! We'll be friends, and Madeira will be lovely –" But she knew, as they walked slowly back to the absorbed group under the coloured umbrellas, that love – even a sudden romantic attraction – did not die to order.

Driving back to Casablanca through the blazing afternoon, she wondered if she would always be emotionally tied to Grant.

"People don't keep on loving the first one," she told herself. "He's years older than me, and he'll probably marry a pretty American girl. It would be natural. I can't marry anyway, for years and years, especially as dancing will always come first. No, I *know* I shall never marry Grant, but I can't get over him. I just go on missing him and wanting him. If I could just hear his voice –" And for a moment, in that hot Moroccan taxi, her longing was almost unbearable.

Yet she couldn't wish that she had never met Grant, and the only hope seemed to be that he had promised that he would see her again. There was even a chance that he might work in London for a time.

They sailed from Casablanca at eleven o'clock that night, and Drina was out on A Deck in her pyjamas as the lights slipped farther and farther away.

After that there was one more day at sea and on Tuesday morning they steamed into Funchal Bay, so early that the high, tapering peaks of the island were lost in the morning mist. Brown-skinned men and boys came out to meet them in rowing-boats and dived for coins in the deep, clear water.

"That's our hotel," said Mr Chester, joining Drina on deck before breakfast. "That big building on the cliff over there."

It was sad to eat a last hurried meal on the ship that had grown so familiar, but exciting to go ashore. The quay was white and shadeless in the sun, but the avenues of the town were tree-shaded, and as they climbed away from the white buildings – the Governor's Palace, once a fortress and built in the sixteenth century, looked Moorish and most impressive on the waterfront – the breeze had a hint of freshness and sweet smells of flowers and the sea. Drina, staring out of the taxi windows at pink and white villas on one side and thickly planted trees with long, upthrusting green leaves on the other, gave a sudden cry:

"Gracious! They're bananas! How fantastic!"

"You've only seen them in shops and on street barrows," said her grandfather, much amused.

"But of course. Oh, there's a lorry-load! Green bananas, and all the leaves, and a man asleep on top."

"You'll see that sight often. Here we are, almost at the hotel."

The taxi swung through a gateway into a garden shaded with palm trees and tall, sub-tropical shrubs, and a white-uniformed porter ushered them into a cool entrance hall.

Their rooms faced the bay and the white curve of the town and Drina was delighted that hers had a balcony that overhung the cliff. Down below were more sub-tropical shrubs and great masses of bougainvillaea, turning bright brown in the August heat.

The great white ship still lay at anchor on the bright

blue water, and the white buildings and then small red-roofed houses rose up and up on the encircling hills. She could see terraced vineyards at a great height, but the bare rocks and the highest peaks were still hidden in the mist.

"It's one of the most beautiful places I've ever seen," she said, roaming into her grandparents' room. "But it hasn't quite the – the astonishment of being in Africa."

"I expect you'll get to love it," said Mr Chester.

"I love it already. I'm ready to love anywhere as hot and flowery as this. May I go out as soon as I've unpacked? Jasper's coming to the hotel and we're going to meet Carol. We want to see the open-air theatre in the gardens and the proper theatre, and there's a short rehearsal at eleven-thirty. The first performance is only two days away."

Mrs Chester sighed.

"That Jasper seems very devoted."

"I'm afraid he is," said Drina, smiling.

Mrs Chester glanced at her, rather taken aback.

"Well, he seems a well brought up boy."

But when Drina had rushed away to unpack she added: "I don't want her to have boyfriends yet. I *thought* he was following her about –"

"My dear, he isn't the first."

"Not the first? You aren't counting Jan Williams or Mark Playford, are you? Or even young Igor Dominick? Because I'm quite sure –"

"No, I wasn't, though Igor isn't so young any more – except in relation to his father – and I think he is attracted. I was thinking of Grant Rossiter."

This time Mrs Chester was more than taken aback.

"What utter rubbish, James! He's years older than Drina. He must be twenty by now. He thought of her as just a child."

"He may have done, up to a point, but Drina was very taken with him. And don't forget they met again in Paris."

"That was an accident. Or at least I always assumed it was. She thinks of nothing but her dancing."

He said no more. It might only have done harm, and, after all, Drina rarely mentioned Grant. It was possible that he was mistaken.

Meanwhile Drina unpacked, rather sketchily, thrust her practice clothes, shoes and a towel into a bag, and went eagerly down the broad staircase to the vast, cool entrance hall. Passing the desk, she saw the clerk holding out some letters. He said in English:

"These are for Mr Chester. If you are going out I will have them sent up —"

"No, I'll take them." The letters had been readdressed from the London flat, as she saw with some surprise.

"Were they on our ship?"

"Some of the mail comes by plane," he said smiling.

Drina turned slowly back up the stairs. The top letter had come from Switzerland. The first postmark said "Lugano" and bore the name of what seemed to be a business firm. Italian sounding surnames and two words – Drina, who read and spoke Italian, translated them without difficulty into "estate agents". Why *on earth* was her grandfather getting a letter from an estate agent in the Ticino?

She knocked and handed them in and saw his gaze fly to the top letter. Mrs Chester was also staring at it. She said quickly:

"Thank you, Drina. Now do mind the sun."

Drina went downstairs once again and there was Jasper in the hall. They went out into the sunshine. Walking along the rather narrow road, in the shadow of a high wall, only half-listening to Jasper's chatter, she puzzled uneasily over the letter. "Something brewing," Jenny had said. But what *could* be brewing, unless it was something to do with a drastic change of living plans? But Switzerland ... No, that was silly. It must be some business acquaintance: her grandfather knew all kinds of people in many countries.

She put the small worry firmly out of her mind and walked on with Jasper, more rapidly, towards the top of the wide and attractive Avenida do Infante. They paused occasionally to gaze at the masses of green bananas growing so low down on the dumpy, long-leaved little trees. Bananas! Drina thought. Very odd! And how very sweet everywhere smelled ... glimpses of brilliantly blue sea ... flower-hung walls ... elegant villas, with wrought-iron balconies and gates.

Jasper and Drina walked briskly along the Avenida Arriaga, which seemed to be the town's main street, with shady trees in the middle and the Cathedral at the far end. There was a cheerful morning bustle and many sights that Drina found strange or interesting. Little carts with canopies and drawn by bullocks went past, each carrying two or three rather self-conscious-looking holiday-makers. It seemed a pity to use bullocks: Drina was an animal-lover. But they looked sleek and well enough fed.

This main street of Funchal was hung with flags, as the waterfront had been, and several notices advertised the various events of the Festival. There was one advertising the Lingeraux Company just outside the public gardens, and, after wandering up some steep, flower-bordered paths, they found themselves close to the open-air theatre. It had a fair-sized stage and quite a large audience-space, in a semi-circle. Around the outside of the semi-circle, where there were long wooden seats against the high hedge of the gardens, men were building elaborate structures with interwoven branches of yew – no, it must be cypress, Drina thought. Something like that. One was finished and it made a very attractive bower. There were little lanterns strung over the top of it.

"I know!" she said to Jasper. "They're meant to be boxes. For the more important people. What a pretty idea!"

One of the workmen saw her interested glances and told her something in Portugese. After a moment she grasped the one word "flowers" and saw what he meant. Later there would be flowers entwined amongst the green branches.

It was all enchanting as well as exciting and they went on eagerly to meet Carol standing by a little fountain.

After that Drina was very much occupied until lunchtime, for Carol insisted on hurrying her off to the shops, where they spent a great many escudos on delightful articles of Madeira embroidery. Drina bought a kind of holdall, very light and useful, made of red and white woolwork on black, a peasant doll and a black lace mantilla. The latter was so beautiful but cost such a lot, that she retreated hastily, leaving Carol to buy another doll and a large bright scarf.

Later they joined the others and they all went along to the municipal theatre, Drina by then rather nervous in case Madame should not be pleased with her dancing after all.

They rehearsed part of the last act of *Casse Noisette*, and it was so hot that, before very long, the sweat poured off them, but there was not even time to think about it. Drina knew the Waltz of the Flowers and it did not take her long to fit herself into the dance. Madame seemed quite pleased and said that there were some extra costumes and one could be altered for her if it should be too big. Then she arranged for Drina and Carol to have a rehearsal of *Twentieth Century Serenade* at six that evening, when it might be a little cooler, and dismissed them.

Drina took a taxi back to the hotel and that afternoon Jasper, Carol and some of the others came to bathe in its private pool at the foot of the cliffs. The afternoon rehearsal went off quite well and Carol had soon grasped what was required of her in Drina's simple but effective little ballet.

"A few more rehearsals," said Madame, joining them when they had been working for some time, "and it will be quite good. You can wear almost any loose, pale dresses. That pink one you wore one night on the ship, Drina. And Carol has a similar one in blue."

"But do you really think it will be good enough, Madame?" Drina asked nervously.

"Of course I do, my dear. It's charming. And we shan't need it for a little while. For the open-air performances, I think."

After dinner that evening the Chesters and Drina had their coffee on the big terrace that overhung the cliff, and dusk came quickly. As the daylight died, lights sprang out in Funchal and lay like stars all over the mountains. Funchal itself gleamed and glowed, for there were extra lights and coloured lanterns because of the Festival, curving in brilliant strings all along the waterfront.

It was hot and still and very, very beautiful, and the sound of music rose from the town, where there was a concert in the gardens. The *Balmoral* had sailed while they were at dinner and already the cabin on A Deck seemed far in the past.

Madeira, now, was the reality.

5

Jasper and Drina

By the time that two or three days had passed Drina was quite at home in Funchal. She loved the old parts of the town, where the pink and cream and white buildings were close together in the narrow cobbled lanes. She loved the pretty, dark-haired children, the smiling people in the shops, and most of all, the unchanging warmth, sunlight and blue sea. She liked the cool, candle-lit gloom of the Cathedral and the other churches ... the climbing roads ... the beauty of the encircling mountains.

She did, of course, mean to see more of Madeira than just Funchal; she particularly longed to go to Terreiro da Lucta for the wonderful view and then the thrilling toboggan run downhill. But exploring farther afield would have to wait for a while, as rehearsals took up part of the day, though usually in the early morning and early evening because of the heat. In between, they explored the environs of Funchal and spent a good deal of time bathing in the deliciously warm water.

After two days on the island Drina was so brown that her appearance was very striking. But then they were all sun-tanned, and, as Carol said sadly, it looked odd on the fair ones.

"I think it looks *better*," Drina argued, for she always admired any colouring but her own. She often regretted that she had not inherited her mother's red hair.

Mr and Mrs Chester spent a good deal of time relaxing on the shady hotel terrace or in the garden. Mr Chester looked very much better and seemed almost his old self, and Mrs Chester's mood was unusually sunny. She seemed quite resigned to the fact that Drina was so often in the company of the younger dancers, though insisting that she should return on time for meals.

"I want to see you a few times a day, just to make sure that you're all right. If you're late, I shall worry."

This was a nuisance, but Drina took it cheerfully.

She particularly enjoyed going to the British Country Club of which she and her grandparents were temporary members. She loved the cool, shuttered building, with its shady veranda. It stood in several acres of sub-tropical gardens, and she was often to be found walking up the narrow, high-walled lane towards the gates.

There were other temporary members of the Club during that August festival and she found it very fascinating to watch – and even to meet – some of the other performers, amongst them well-known singers and the principals of the South British Shakespearean Company. Cécile Barreux and Michael Mann were also members and they were always very pleasant to Drina, a fact that she much appreciated, for she felt herself very unimportant. She borrowed books from the library there and sometimes lay sprawled under a shady tree, reading. But, on the whole, there was not much time for books, with so many other appealing pastimes. The warm water drew her at least twice a day and was one of her greatest pleasures.

Jasper rather resented her membership of the Club, but shook his head when she suggested that he should join.

"I don't think I'd better. It's different for you, staying

at the hotel. I don't believe that Cécile Barreux would like it.''

"Oh, rubbish!" said Drina. "Anyone can join while they're here." But she did not really want to press the point. She continued to like Jasper, and in many ways they had much in common, but his so obvious devotion rather embarrassed her.

"He has got it badly!" said Carol once, perfectly kindly. "And I think it really is the first time, too. He's a self-contained, reserved boy in many ways. I gather you don't feel the same about him?"

"No, I like him, but –"

"Someone else?" Carol gave her a shrewd look.

"Yes. It's hopeless – quite hopeless – but there *is* someone else." In a way it was a relief to talk about it. She had kept the whole thing bottled-up for so long, except for that talk with Miss Whiteway in Paris.

They were stretched out by the pool and Jasper was still swimming.

"Why is it hopeless? You're most attractive; more than that. You've got something."

"Because he's a good deal older and he lives in New York." And then, lying there in the hot Madeira sunshine, Drina told her briefly about Grant and found her an understanding listener.

"Will it go, do you think? I once read that love can't survive long separation and great distance."

"I don't know," said Carol. "Probably only when you meet someone else."

"But I don't even *want* to."

Drina was never to know that, almost at that very moment, on a humid morning in New York (it was afternoon in Madeira), Grant Rossiter was sitting at his office desk, wishing that lunchtime would come and thinking of Drina. From the thirty-ninth floor window of the tall block where his father's firm had their offices there was a view towards the United Nations Secretariat and the East River, but he was not seeing that at all. He was seeing a girl with swinging black hair walking through the soft maytime woods of Versailles ... and then again, on that last evening, when he put her into a taxi and drove back with her to her hotel near the Gare du Nord. He saw her tense face, her lower lip held between her teeth and the lights of Paris drawing a faint sheen out of her dark hair. Then her face again as she looked up at him in the hotel lobby, as they said goodbye.

So young; and there was her dancing. What was the good of it, he asked himself for the hundredth time. Why allow himself to be haunted still by her soft, English voice and by the face that had many times shown him all too clearly how she felt? Other girls had fallen for Grant Rossiter since his early teens, and he had by no means been immune himself, but there was a quality about this English girl that refused to be dismissed.

"I guess I must really be in love," he thought hopelessly. "And it's just no good, even if I go to London next year. She's only a kid and she has her dancing. She's going to be a great ballerina. I'm darn sure of that."

And he attacked his work fiercely for another quarter of an hour, then went out to lunch.

On their second evening in Madeira they all went to see the Shakespearean Company, and on the third night the Lingeraux Company gave their first performance in the Municipal Theatre. Mr Chester had taken seats for this, saying that they must be there to see Drina dance, and for once Drina was not nervous. It was something new to be only one of many in the Waltz of the Flowers, and she was glad that the first performance of her own ballet was not until the following evening. Then she *would* be nervous, dreadfully so, though there would be no terrifying London or Paris critics and, people seemed out to enjoy themselves.

Two days later Drina wrote to Rose:

The first performance was fun, because the audience was such a good one and it was clear at once that they liked the Lingeraux. Of course I only danced in Casse Noisette *and that came at the end. I watched the rest from the wings, Cécile Barreux and Michael Mann are awfully good, especially in the pas de deux from* Don Quixote, *but the Company as a whole isn't up to the Dominick. Rather ragged corps, I think, but then of course it isn't the whole company and the conditions aren't ideal. Quite a small stage.*

The next evening we gave a performance in the open-air theatre, and I was scared stiff over Twentieth Century Serenade. *But Carol is really very good and I needn't have been scared, because the audience seemed to love it. And the whole thing was magical: such a hot and windless night, with sweet smells and the sky thick with stars. They have built little boxes decked with flowers and coloured lanterns, and the lights glow through the darkness.*

Oh, Rose, I do know how lucky I am. Madeira is the most enchanting place. Today several of us hired a taxi and went to Camara de Lobos and some other little villages. Funchal is ringed by mountains, and nearly all the roads climb. Some of them are quite alarming.

Earlier in the year the island must be even more beautiful, but there are still a lot of flowers. Little cottages smothered in hydrangea hedges, and terraced vineyards, and banana plantations. And the coast is wild and rocky, with always the blue, blue sea.

The children and the young girls are beautiful – some of the men, I think, look more like Mexicans than Portuguese.

There are such a lot of fascinating things to buy: all kinds of embroidery, which is one of the island's main industries, and lace and cane furniture. They do most of the work in the cottages and you can often see girls and their mothers sitting out in the little gardens, busy with their embroidery.

I shall be terribly sorry to leave, and some day I'd like to come back. But life is really very difficult – so many new places to see, and so many old ones that I long to see again.

Grandfather seems much better, almost his old self, and Granny is very amiable, on the whole. I am not really quite easy in my mind, and yet I keep on hoping I'm making something out of nothing. Jenny said she thought that something was brewing and there have been one or two little incidents that I'm trying to forget. It's no use asking Granny, anyway, and I don't like to worry Grandfather, though it seems to me that he looks at me oddly sometimes. I wonder often if they're making plans for next winter that I won't like. People our age are so helpless – how often I've said that. I wish I were grown up and could make my own plans and not be so dependent.

Meanwhile, I bathe in this lovely warm water, and roam and dance. There is a boy called Jasper, one of the youngest members of the Lingeraux. He's rather good-looking and so nice and he follows me round in a devoted way. I don't quite know what to do about him, so I just try to be natural and pleasant. I'm not in the least in love with him, though how I wish I were in this romantic setting.

Here are Carol and the others coming to bathe, so must stop.

Love from
Drina

Very soon people recognised Drina in the streets of Funchal and often stopped to tell her how much they had enjoyed her little ballet.

So the warm days passed happily. When there was no performance in the evenings, Carol, Jasper and some of the others usually went to a concert or else just strolled along the waterfront in the lamp-lit dusk. Sometimes Drina and Jasper walked alone and Jasper was always trying to organise this, but more often they were in a group.

On several occasions they went for excursions by bus or taxi and that way Drina saw most of the island, delighting in the wild mountains and never really alarmed by the sometimes precipitous roads. She made the descent by toboggan – a definitely slightly alarming, but also exciting experience – and loved the more remote little villages clinging to the rocky coast or climbing the bare hills.

It really was an enchanted time and the days passed so quickly that, almost before she realised it, they had only three or four days left in Funchal. The Lingeraux Company was staying on for a week longer than the Chesters and Drina, and this made Drina a little sad. It made Jasper sad, too, for very different reasons.

"I don't see why you can't persuade your grandparents to stay longer," he grumbled one morning, when he had firmly collected Drina from her hotel.

"I don't think we could if we wanted to. We only

booked at the last minute and we'd probably never get cabins on another ship. No, I can't do anything about it. But I shall hate to go," Drina said, with a faint sigh. They were walking down the now very familiar Avenida do Infante. "I have loved it. I wish I could always live in the sun."

"But we can meet in London? You do promise that?"

"Oh, we're sure to meet sometimes," Drina said, and found her hand in his.

"I wish you'd say it as though you mean it!"

"Of course I mean it. But I did tell you, I'm terribly busy."

They were nearly down by the waterfront when Jasper said:

"I've arranged to hire a little motor-boat. You said the other day you'd like to go out in a boat."

Drina looked startled. She had said it casually, in conversation, and had not really thought much about it.

"I don't believe Granny would be very keen. Just us two, do you mean?"

"Yes. It's only a *little* boat."

"But wouldn't it hold Carol as well? She'd love it, you know."

"They've gone off somewhere by bus." He was beginning to look really hurt, and she said no more, but followed him rather reluctantly towards some steps, where a number of small boats were moored. The boat's owner rose from a seat in the shade when he saw them and ushered them down the steps with some ceremony, showing very white teeth in a pleased smile.

"Lovely boat … lovely day. Happy time with pretty young lady."

"But can you manage a motor-boat?"

"Of course," said Jasper, with great assurance. "I've often hired one in other places."

"I shall have to be back in time for lunch, you know, or Granny will be cross. She does insist on me being back on time."

"You'll be back in time," said Jasper, rather crossly, handing her a scarlet cushion. But once they were out on the calm blue waters of the bay he grew happy again and there was no doubt that it was delightful. The little boat chugged steadily southwards and Drina trailed her fingers in the water.

Funchal, a little dimmed in the heat haze, climbed the mountains, and they could really see the shape of it now. There had hardly been time to savour the view on that early morning when they disembarked from the *Balmoral*.

Jasper turned the boat in presently towards the coast and they landed on a tiny beach that was so inaccessible as to be almost deserted. Drina wandered about searching the rock pools for shells, and then they sat and talked. Jasper was an amusing and interesting companion and his sun-tanned face was very animated.

But at last Drina glanced at her watch and said that she really must get back. They scrambled into the boat again and Jasper started the engine. It gave a few rather alarming phuts and seemed reluctant, but presently burst into life and they set off again round the headland into Funchal Bay. The blue haze had thickened and the pale-coloured buildings showed only dimly now.

It was at this point, when they were still well out in the bay, that the engine began to cough and very rapidly it died.

A rather appalled silence fell on the little boat, then Jasper said:

"Don't worry. I'm sure it's nothing. I'll have her going again in no time."

"I definitely hope so," said Drina, for it was already

growing late and she knew that she would be in disgrace if she were not back in time for lunch. For one thing her grandmother was strict over looking clean and tidy for meals and she felt very hot and grubby. She would need a few minutes to wash and do her hair.

The calm water was alarmingly empty of small craft, but a big ship was coming up from the south, still some distance away.

Jasper bent over the little engine without another word.

6

More Trouble for Drina

For ten minutes or more Jasper tinkered with the engine, muttering:

"Plenty of petrol ... What on earth can it be? Don't worry, Drina she'll go in a minute."

Meanwhile, they were drifting gently, fortunately not out of the bay but slightly towards Funchal. The thought of the vast Atlantic was an alarming one and Drina began to wonder what would have happened to them if there had been a wind blowing away from the island.

Even so it was a big enough problem and she knew very well that her grandmother would be furious if she learned what had happened. And if she were late for lunch the story would probably have to be told.

"I knew I shouldn't come," she thought glumly, watching Jasper's bent back. His thin shirt was sticking to his shoulder-blades, for the sun blazed down. Drina was thankful for her shady sunhat but even so it was unpleasantly like being grilled. For the first time since leaving England she began to wish heartily that it were a little cooler.

"I could take off my shirt and wave to that ship," Jasper said suddenly.

"They wouldn't see you. It's still a long way away. They'd just think you were sending a greeting if they did."

"But it's coming in. It's a cruise ship. I heard it was expected."

"On a rather wide curve, though. It's going to miss us by quite a distance."

This was patently true and Jasper bent again to the engine. After another few minutes it sprang rather uncertainly into life and he shouted with triumph.

Drina remained silent as they began very slowly to move towards Funchal, and it was no great surprise when the engine coughed again and fell silent. But they had made some progress and the waterfront now did not look so alarmingly far away.

They sat there in gloomy silence until Jasper burst out:

"I really am sorry, Drina. I don't know what it is. The man swore that the boat was fine – almost new."

"It's all right; not your fault." But by now Drina was feeling sick with the glare of the sun, the dazzle of the water and her deep anxiety. At that very moment she should have been at the hotel, which she could see tantalisingly on its cliff in the distance.

Quite a long time passed, during which the big liner moved majestically into the bay. It was Drina who gave the relieved shout this time.

"The boats are going out to her!"

As when the *Balmoral* had arrived, small rowing-boats carrying brown-skinned men and boys were going to meet the ship. Twenty or thirty craft began to string out on the waters of the bay and some were obviously going to pass near enough to the becalmed motor-boat to be within hailing distance.

Drina began to shout and wave her hat and Jasper

joined in. At first it seemed that the men of Funchal thought they were being funny, but presently one boat detached itself and came towards them. In it were two young men, both grinning widely.

Then followed a small pantomime, and they soon grasped that the engine wouldn't work and that the Englishman and the pretty girl wanted a tow back to Funchal. But they seemed in no hurry to come to the rescue until Jasper brandished some money.

One of them said:

"More!"

"It's robbery!" Jasper cried indignantly. "It would take them hours to earn this much diving for coins."

"You'll have to, though." Drina was almost frantic by this time. "Here, I've got plenty of money. I'll pay half."

"No, you won't! This was my idea and I'll pay for it. All right, then," he added to the brown-skinned, still grinning brigands.

They might not understand the words, but he held the extra notes in his hand, with no intention of parting with the money until they set foot on the quay.

There was a rope in the motor-boat and this was attached to the rowing-boat. Both pairs of light oars were soon moving rhythmically and they progressed slowly towards the waterfront.

The arrival of a ship was always an event, and there were plenty of people about to see the arrival of the crippled motor-boat and her red-faced, thoroughly upset passengers. The boat's owner was there and Jasper cried furiously:

"I wish I could speak Portuguese! I could do better than in English, though he does speak some. Drina, I'm really sorry –"

"It's all right. Sorry, I must fly!" Drina leaped ashore the moment it was possible and fled up the steps, leaving Jasper to part with his money and complain to the boat's owner as best he could. It seemed obvious that he would do it with considerable verve and a wealth of gesture.

She ran across the hot concrete towards the waiting taxis and flung herself into the first one. Sinking down on the hot back seat, she was conscious that her head was throbbing and that she felt sicker than ever. Lunch would be over and her grandmother was certain to be both worried and angry.

In fact, Mrs Chester was out in the drive when the taxi swept through the gates and she came forward at once.

"Drina, where *have* you been? I was really worried. No, I'll pay." And she hastily dealt with the driver, while Drina stood dazed on the gravel.

Mrs Chester put her hand on her arm.

"What on earth happened? Why didn't you telephone? What's the matter with you?"

"Just a bit – odd," Drina managed to gasp. Then she was in the blessed coolness of the entrance hall, where her grandfather was sitting in a deep chair. He looked relieved to see her, but at once grew anxious again.

"What is it? Is she ill?"

"I don't know," said Mrs Chester. "She says she feels odd. To much sun, by the look of her."

"And I was so worried that you'd be worried," Drina got out.

The hall was swinging round her and she never knew how she got to her room.

"Are you going to be sick?" her grandmother asked, helping her to the bed.

"No. Yes. I don't know. This is – is just silly."

Mrs Chester saw her settled against the soft pillows and wrung out her face cloth in cold water.

"I'll put this on your forehead and fetch my eau-de-Cologne. Just lie still and maybe the sickness will pass off."

She half-closed the shutters and went away, returning in a moment with the eau-de-Cologne. By then Drina was feeling a little better and the acute nausea was passing off.

"Granny, I'm so sorry! I didn't mean to worry you –"

"You seem to have got yourself into a fine state," Mrs Chester said grimly. "Maybe it's my fault for insisting that you get back in time. But I still don't see why you couldn't telephone. It may be a foreign country, but I'm sure you could have managed it."

"Oh, of course, but it was impossible –"

"How do you mean, impossible?"

"Because I was out in a boat with Jasper and the engine failed. It was very hot and I got worked up –"

Mrs Chester grunted indignantly, but it seemed clear that Drina was better left in silence just then.

"You may tell me later. I don't know what you were doing going out in a motor-boat. You might have known I shouldn't like it. Go to sleep now, and you'd better stay here for the rest of the day. I'll have some tea sent up to you later. You don't want lunch."

"Oh – no!" The very thought made her feel bad again.

"I wonder if I should call a doctor –"

Drina lay there alone for some time, gradually relaxing, as she remembered thankfully that there was no performance that evening. The last show in which she would dance was on the following evening in the public gardens.

Finally she slept and was awakened by the arrival of tea, carried by a waiter who was followed by her grandmother.

Mrs Chester poured out and handed Drina her cup

and some thin sandwiches.

"Are you feeling better now? Did you sleep?"

"Yes, Granny. Both."

"That young Jasper came up and apologised. He took all the blame, but I'm afraid I was rather short with him. The two of you shouldn't have gone off in a boat. I shudder to think what would have happened if you'd drifted out to sea."

Drina shuddered to think of it, too. They had been very lucky.

Drina was quite all right again by the next morning, but Mrs Chester was adamant, insisting that she must sit in the shady garden all morning. She and Mr Chester had arranged to go for a drive with some other English people staying in the hotel and she would have preferred to cancel it.

"Oh, you go, Granny," Drina urged. "I really will write letters and read. Carol may come up and we'll just talk."

So the Chesters went off and Drina spent a peaceful hour, until both Carol and Jasper arrived. The three of them lived over again the adventure in the boat and Jasper was still subdued and apologetic.

But he was happier by the time that he and Carol left to have lunch at the guest-house.

The Chesters arrived back rather late for lunch and Mr Chester was confessing to a headache.

"I don't care for high places and the sun *was* very bright: so little shade. I won't have coffee. I think I'll go and have a rest."

Drina and her grandmother had their coffee out on the high terrace and it was then that Mrs Chester learned that Jasper had been around that morning.

"He's a nice boy and I've really nothing against him,

except that he does seem rather possessive about you. I hope you don't regard him as your boyfriend?" She used the last word with slight distaste, as though it belonged to an unfamiliar language.

Drina grinned. She felt quite light-hearted now.

"Oh, no, Granny, I don't. I do like him, though. I expect I shall see him occasionally in London next winter."

To her surprise a strange expression showed on her grandmother's face.

"I hardly think so," she said and then looked as though she would have given much to take the words back.

In a second Drina's light-heartedness had gone and all her vague doubts fused into a gigantic certainty of disaster. She stared at her grandmother and must have gone pale in spite of her tan, for Mrs Chester said quickly:

"What's the matter? Why do you look like that?"

"You've *got* to tell me, Granny! I *must* know. You're keeping something from me."

"There's no 'got' about it," Mrs Chester said stiffly, but she looked dismayed and her voice, amazingly, shook a little.

"No, but – look, I'm not a child any more. You oughtn't to shut me out. There *is* something and it's to do with next winter."

"Yes," Mrs Chester said slowly and very reluctantly. "There is something, though I had not meant to tell you until we got home. You say you are not a child, so please prove it by listening sensibly and trying to help me."

"I will – of course. Is it trouble, then?"

"You may think so, and yet many girls would jump at the chance. We – we have made certain plans for the winter. You see, the doctors absolutely refuse to let your grandfather stay in London. They say that if he does he may not – may not live to see the spring." Her normally controlled voice shook again.

Drina was appalled on the two counts, but her grandfather's welfare came uppermost in those first moments of shock.

"Granny, how terrible! I didn't know – I had no idea."

"But if he winters in a better climate he may live for many years. That is why ... our plans ... we have taken a villa in Switzerland from the third week in September."

Now there was a singing in Drina's ears and a feeling of such black despair in her heart that she scarcely saw the tense face opposite to her.

"The Dominick ... Oh, the Dominick! What is going to happen to *me*?" But she did not speak the words aloud. They would not have come.

Mrs Chester went on more evenly:

"From the financial point of view it will be rather a struggle, as we haven't so much money now that your grandfather has retired. This naturally doesn't affect you, as you have your own and some of it can be used for your education and so on. The villa sounds a charming place. It's in the Ticino, the Italian-speaking part of Switzerland, not far from Lugano. We are giving up the Westminster flat, but later we may take another one. We will have to see how your grandfather goes on. It seems now that he will want to to return to England in the spring."

"But, Granny –" It came out in a croak. Drina gasped and went on: "Shall I – would Miss Whiteway have me? Or could I board out, as the twins do?"

Mrs Chester was silent for quite a time, staring unseeingly at the waters of the bay. When she spoke it was to say:

"Drina, this is going to be hard for you. Don't think I don't realise it. I *know* all you will feel, but I am going to ask you to do this for both our sakes. Your grandfather has been strongly against it, yet he would worry all the time if we left you in London. And after your escapade yesterday –"

"Granny, that isn't fair!" It came in an agonised cry.

Mrs Chester looked a little ashamed.

"Perhaps not. Anyway, it couldn't really be with Miss Whiteway, as she is away so much, and you are too young to be on your own – neither of us would have an easy moment."

"The twins –"

"There are two of them, and if their parents like to risk it that is their affair. I personally could never agree until you are at least a senior student. You still aren't very strong ... we should both worry ourselves to death. Your grandfather would bear that, for your sake, but it would harm him. You must see that. So I want you to tell him cheerfully and willingly that you will enjoy a winter in Switzerland. I am asking that of you, the first really hard thing I have ever asked you to do."

"No," Drina thought, "you asked – no, you *made* me – leave Willerbury. That was the first hard thing." But then she did become aware of the pain and anxiety in her grandmother's face and realised, with a sharp stab of sympathy, how deep her worry must be over the person who was nearest to her in the world.

"But, Granny, what about my *dancing*?"

Mrs Chester said slowly:

"I have consulted Mr Dominick and Miss Volonaise. They understand fully. They have promised that the fact of missing some months at the Dominick shall make no difference, so long as you pass your exams in the summer. We will really definitely come back in April for your sake. They seem sure that you will be accepted as a senior student when the time comes. Meanwhile we are also arranging for your dancing to be carried on. Have you forgotten that your cousin Antonia now goes to school near Lugano?"

"Yes. I – I had. But it's a finishing school, not – not a ballet school." The black despair was still there, but she tried to speak calmly.

"Some of the girls learn ballet."

"But they won't be professionals – ever. How could I learn with a lot of – of –?"

Mrs Chester smiled faintly at the scorn in her voice.

"They have a first-class teacher from La Scala, Milan. She travels to Lugano twice a week. She really is a well-known teacher and the Dominick people think very, very highly of her. They even say that a change of teacher may do more good than harm."

"But I have a lesson every *day*."

"That can't be arranged, but there is an excellent studio at this school and you could practise every day. You would have your lesson alone, too, as the others certainly won't be up to your standard."

"I – I should like to see Antonia. But – oh, Granny!"

"We plan to have a few days in Milan," Mrs Chester went on, "visiting your Italian grandmother. I thought you'd like that, and she and I really should meet again now that all the unpleasantness is behind us." The unpleasantness she referred to concerned the fight between the two grandmothers to bring up the orphaned baby Drina.

"That would be – nice." Then Drina could stand it no longer. She rose, abandoning her half-drunk and now stone cold coffee.

"Don't come! I'm all right." And she fled to the silence and blessed privacy of her room.

7

The Last Performance

Drina flung back the shutters and stood staring blindly out at the dark blue water, the bright colours in the deep ravine and at the buildings climbing the mountains. It was a scene already grown very familiar, but if it had been quite new she would not have noticed it.

She was breathing strangely and was almost unable to swallow. Shock, fear for her grandfather and horror at her own future seemed to have made her only half-alive. She gripped the sill and fought with herself, trying to think and finding it impossible.

Deep quiet was all about her and few sounds came up from the town, where the siesta was well under way, almost over. For they had had lunch late and it was now well past three o'clock.

Gradually uppermost came her own possibly selfish but very natural suffering. The Dominick had not always been perfect lately, as it had seemed in the early days, but it was the only school she wanted … the only school she had ever expected to know now. To be away for a whole winter, two long terms, was a blow that she had never imagined. It had been bad enough when she was sent to Chalk Green while her grandparents were in Australia. She had thought of Chalk Green as "exile", but it had been part of the Dominick and she had, in the end, learned to love it. But a totally unknown finishing school in Switzerland, even though it would mean being with her Italian cousin, Antonia, would be impossible ... dreadful beyond words. To be away from Red Lion Square – her heart gave a wild leap, for when she came back again the Dominick School would no longer be in Red Lion Square at all, but in the new building on the South Bank. That had been goodbye, in July, when she, Rose and Ilonka walked out so casually.

The silence and inaction were both suddenly unbearable. Drina snatched up her sunhat and bag and rushed downstairs and out into the garden. Sitting under a tree not far from the drive was her grandmother and she had seen her. Drina ran to her and said stumblingly:

"I've *got* to be alone to think about it. Please don't worry, Granny. Make some excuse to Grandfather. I'll do what you say ... I'll do it as well as I possibly can, so that he doesn't know. But leave me alone *now*!"

Then she was gone, and Mrs Chester made no attempt to stop her. She really did know that this was tragedy for Drina; in any case it would have been useless to try to follow that fleet-footed dash through the open gates.

But it was too hot to run for long and Drina slowed down after a short while, walking along in the shadow of the familiar high walls. She was not thinking at all and it was a very long time before she became remotely aware of her surroundings. She had been climbing steadily and now she was even higher than a high church. There were vine terraces and little red-roofed houses still, but growing more frequent. And when she stopped at last to rest, panting and dripping wet, the vast view of Funchal and sea and encircling mountains swam in the hard dry light of afternoon.

Presently she went on, for she needed to be away from all people, in a wild, lonely place where she could really think. The vineyards gave place at last to bare rocks and an occasional falling stream and she was quite alone on the Madeira mountains. But on the road there was still a chance of cars and she plunged away up a tiny valley and presently flung herself down in a hollow in the shadow of some overhanging rocks.

Even then, for a long time, she did not think, but half-dozed, lost in drifting, despairing thoughts. And into these thoughts came at last a vision of Jenny when *she* had learned that her old life had ended. Jenny, thin-faced, hard with a grim courage, her voice brittle but determinly cheerful in the presence of her family.

Jenny's life had *ended*; she had seen no way ever to win again her old dreams of an agricultural college and farming. And she might at that very moment be doing a job that she hated.

Drina, suddenly fully awake, looked into her own immediate future and saw that, for most girls, it would not have been bad at all. A trip to Milan, a winter in a warmer climate beside a romantic lake, an expensive finishing school. She had not stopped to ask if she would be a boarder, but it seemed likely. Maybe she would visit her grandparents at weekends. And it was not even as though there would be no dancing at all. There would be the excellent Italian teacher, a studio in which to practise, a chance to perfect her Italian and to see yet more new places.

On the face of it it was not at all tragic. But it would mean not seeing anyone that she knew, none of her friends, for many months. Not Rose, or Ilonka, or Jenny, Miss Whiteway or anyone at all. It would mean, too, being out of reach of the theatre, with no chance of public appearances. The Dominick would go on without her and she would be an exile indeed, probably amongst girls who were mainly older, for she remembered now that Antonia had written something about them being over sixteen.

Now the miseries of a London winter seemed wholly desirable; she would have given anything to know that she would again stand in a bus queue on a sleety morning, shivering in the wind blowing off the river.

But clearly there was no choice, except that she could take it well or badly. And if she took it badly her grandfather would suffer. So she would somehow have to go back and make him believe that she liked the prospect. He understood her; *would* he believe her? Now she could interpret his extra kindness and the anxious looks he had sometimes cast at her.

"I must do it. I must!" she told herself, and with the certain knowledge that the decision was taken, she dozed again, exhausted.

Later she sat up suddenly, bristling with alarm and dawning awareness. The sun had moved round the sky and was now shining full on her. The whole vast landscape was stark under the blazing blue sky. It must be late!

When she saw that it was already well after six o'clock her heart leaped sickeningly. She sprang to her feet in a worse panic than the one that had gone before. For the show started at eight. Her own ballet was early in the programme, too.

Scrambling down to the road, in imminent danger of twisting an ankle, she realised with shame that, for the first time in her life, she had *forgotten* a performance. She had been asleep on a mountain when she ought to have been thinking of the evening. She never had dinner before a performance, just milk and sandwiches, but even so she was going to be late. She could see the whole of Funchal outspread now, even the roof of her hotel, but it was a long way away and she would only be ill again if she ran all the way through the hot evening. Even if she did run she would still be late, for she must certainly go back to the hotel first and reassure her grandparents.

She began to walk downhill, telling herself savagely that it served her right. For in Madeira, for the first time ever, she had not really taken dancing seriously. It had all been fun, after those first two performances of her own ballet. She had danced light-heartedly, undisturbed in any way, and now here was the result of it.

Never, never again, she vowed, as she plodded on, her legs aching a little on the steep downward gradient, would she let it happen. Dust flew up from under her sandals and made her sneeze and everything was now so like a nightmare that she could hardly believe in her own reality. If she were late, Madame Lingeraux would be furious ... everyone would be upset ... and she herself would never get over the shame of it.

When she reached the first house she passed an old man leading a bullock cart. He grinned at her and spoke a greeting, but Drina scarcely saw him. She was praying for a car to overtake her. This was a rough road, but she was dimly aware that a few cars had passed her going up.

Then, miraculously, she heard one coming, but when she turned round it was crowded to the doors and the occupants merely waved cheerfully. It went on round a bend, leaving a cloud of dust.

When she looked at her watch again, it was twenty to seven and she still had a long way to go. With the best will in the world she would not reach the hotel much before half-past, and she would be hot, hungry and very dirty, in no state to dance, even if her grandmother would let her shower and leave immediately.

Then suddenly she heard another car and the miracle had happened. In it, apart from the driver, were only Michael Mann and Cécile Barreux and it was already stopping. Cécile leaned out, staring in dismay at the face that was streaked with long-dried tears and a pattern of dust marks.

"Drina, my dear, what are you doing up here? What's the *matter*?"

Drina scrambled into the car, weak with relief.

"Oh, it really is a miracle! I had a problem and I came up here to think. I *forgot* the performance, and –"

The two adults eyed her and then each other.

"Don't try to talk now," said Michael Mann. "Tell us later, some time. We'll get you back."

They were at the hotel in a wonderfully short time, and by then Drina had gathered that they, too, had had rather a nightmare time, for the car had broken down high in the mountains.

"However, we'll all just manage it," said Cécile Barreux comfortingly. "Have a shower and a cool drink and you'll feel much better."

Drina hurried to her room, hoping to avoid being seen until she was cleaner and calmer, and luck favoured her, for she had showered and was wearing her pretty cotton housecoat when there was a tap at the door and Mrs Chester came in. She looked deeply relieved to see her granddaughter.

"There you are! They said at the desk that you were back. I've ordered your milk and sandwiches to be sent up. Are you all right?"

"Yes, Granny, quite all right."

"Then come in and speak to your grandfather. He's just getting ready for dinner."

Drina gathered up all her courage and followed her. Her grandfather eyed her anxiously and she said quickly:

"Hullo, Grandfather! Is your headache better?"

"Yes, quite better. But, Drina –"

"Granny's told me about Switzerland and it's quite all right. I shall love to be with Antonia and so long as I can keep on with my ballet –"

"But are you sure?" he asked, with a mixture of relief and doubt. "I dare say we could get you in with the twins, and Miss Whiteway and Miss Volonaise would keep an eye on you."

Conscious of her grandmother's presence behind her, Drina said:

"Yes, I expect so, but it will be better if I come. I – I would miss you both so much. No, it's all settled and I'm just dying to hear all about the villa and the school. But it'll have to wait now, because I haven't very long."

Back in her room and dressing rapidly, she thought that she had not carried it off badly. Maybe he had not been deceived, but he would just have to be convinced by her future behaviour.

After so much strain and emotion she was very hungry and the sandwiches tasted delicious. A short while later she stepped into a taxi and was carried down towards the town and the public gardens.

It was, like every other night since their arrival in Madeira, warm, starry and most beautiful and the audience that gathered at the open-air theatre wore only the lightest of clothing. Yet Drina found herself shivering as she waited to dance in *Twentieth Century Serenade*. Beside her, Carol whispered:

"What's the matter? I know something is."

"I can't tell you now. It will have to be tomorrow. I shall have all morning and part of the afternoon, anyway. We don't go on board until between seven and eight and sail at eleven."

The ship that had arrived the previous day, the cruise liner, had left at lunchtime. The one that would take the Chesters and Drina back to England was not expected until the following afternoon.

Standing there, watching the *pas de deux* being danced on the little stage and then gazing out into the lantern-lit shadows, Drina was swept with despair again and a feeling of rebellion. Madeira was so lovely … everything had been so perfect … and soon it would be over and the return to England would bring endless problems and upsets in its train. She had not yet really had time to think and plan, but there would only be two weeks or so in which to pack, see her friends and get herself adjusted to the idea of the new life.

The new life! What a terrible thought!

When it was time to go on stage, and the first chords of the *Twentieth Century Serenade* music rang through the warm darkness, she wondered in a small panic if she would be able to dance at all. Then suddenly she *was* dancing and it was, strangely, as if her ballet had a deeper meaning, or perhaps its original meaning had intensified. For it was meant to depict two young girls, unknowing and uncaring at first, then gradually learning the meaning of sorrow and joy – the meaning of living.

Out in the audience Madame Lingeraux did not watch Carol at all, but concentrated on the slim, black-haired figure with the expressive face, and she, at least, was aware that tonight, in the simple ballet, there was an element of great dancing; passion and feeling that were surprising in so young and apparently so inexperienced a girl. Her technique had always been good, but now there was a maturity that was wholly unexpected.

Ivory's daughter! Madame sighed and wished that fate had sent *her* this plum of the ballet world. And she wondered wryly how many members of that probably ill-informed audience would ever look back on this night, realising that the girl who called herself Drina Adams was really Andrina Adamo, daughter of one of the greatest dancers who had ever lived.

She was almost prophetically sure, in those moments when the short ballet moved towards its end, that here would be greatness again and a name that would one day ring round the world.

8

"The Rain in Spain –"

By the time that she met Jasper and Carol the next morning Drina knew rather more about the Swiss plans, including the definite fact that she would be a weekly boarder at the school.

"You can come home on Friday evenings and return on Sunday evening," Mrs Chester said. She was so relieved to have won her point with so little struggle that she was being extra gentle and kind. "The villa sounds a charming place, with a big garden. We have taken it furnished, of course, and our own furniture will go into store in London."

"And *are* all the girls quite old?" The effort to sound happy and interested was almost too much for Drina, but she was managing it somehow.

"I believe so. You must see the prospectus when we get home. The headteacher is an Englishwoman, who formerly taught at a school in the Bernese Oberland, but the school is run for girls of all nationalities. You enjoy meeting foreigners, so you'll like that. They have a fairly general education, but with time given to a great many extras – music, art and languages. Travel, too. The girls are often taken about and groups spend a few days several times a term in Berne or Zurich or other cities.

Actually you will be by far the youngest. Girls are usually over sixteen when they go to the school."

"I very nearly will be sixteen by then."

"Yes, in a few weeks. Some of the girls are almost grown up."

"No boys?" Drina asked, and Mr Chester laughed.

"Certainly not. I fancy that the girls will be rather carefully protected from young men."

"Oh, Grandfather, how silly!"

"You'll have to accept the rules of the school," Mrs Chester said, a little stiffly, then, remembering her gentler role, she added: "Don't tell me you can't live without boys?"

"Well, I suppose I can, but I never have. They're – they're part of life, aren't they?"

"I suppose so," her grandmother agreed, rather reluctantly. She was, in theory, totally against coeducation, but it had worked well enough in Drina's case.

Drina asked a few more questions, then escaped thankfully. When Jasper and Carol arrived, she was sitting on the grass under a palm tree, watching the gates. After their swim she told them the whole story and Jasper was very upset. He had been counting on seeing Drina again during the winter and it was a blow to be told that she was to be removed to the far away Italian-speaking part of Switzerland. The Lingeraux sometimes danced in Zurich or Basle – the Company was very popular in both cities – but Lugano was far from either.

"But they oughtn't to make you go. It's quite wrong. It will ruin your career, and –"

"I don't suppose it will," Drina said sadly. "And there *is* one thing – I never really took it in at the time. The Dominick people have evidently said that I'll certainly be a senior student next year, just so long as I pass my exams, and that's a relief. I never have been quite certain that it would happen. No, I shall have to go and try and live through the time as best I can. I owe it to Grandfather and I suppose to Granny as well. But I shall undoubtedly hate most of it. I'm quite prepared for that."

"But you might *like* it," Carol said tentatively. "Switzerland is such a lovely country and I did go to Lugano once. The lake is beautiful and I liked the town and all the cobbled squares and stone arcades. Morcote, Gandria, Campione; all the little places on the lake. They were heavenly."

"It would be all right for a holiday. I love what I've seen of Switzerland. I once stayed in Kandersteg in the Alps. But – oh, my heart feels like a stone! The Dominick will be *gone* when I get back. And I don't know what my friends will say." They lay luxuriously in the hot sun and Drina thought miserably that soon she would be far away. A few days on the ship and then London again with all her problems. Life was going to be very real and earnest for a while.

So the last hours in Madeira slipped by, the packing was finished and there was nothing more to do except enjoy the last of the sun and familiar scenes. Late that afternoon Drina and Jasper walked along the Avenida Arriaga for the last time and she let him hold her hand. It seemed the least she could do, and in a way it was a comfort to feel that he liked her and was suffering, too, though for a very different reason.

The ship that would carry her away was already in the bay and she returned to the hotel, walking for the last time up the Avenida do Infante, past the banana trees that had surprised her so much at first.

To her surprise most of the Company were down on

the quay to see her off, and Jasper had brought an enormous bouquet. So Drina went aboard clutching the flowers and soon they were arranged in the pleasant cabin that would be her home until they reached Southampton.

Darkness fell softly, and long before they sailed the lights of Funchal sprang out. Drina, alone on the Boat Deck in the hot, windless night, was moved by so much beauty, for from the sea it was almost impossible to tell which were lights and which were stars, so high on the mountains were the little houses. It was really only second to New York at night and she knew that she would always remember it, but the memory would be all tangled up with her present bleak unhappiness.

When at last they sailed, she was still on deck and she continued to stand there for a long time, until they rounded the island and Funchal disappeared.

The ship was to make only one call and that was at Vigo, in Spain. Drina, who had never been to Spain, would normally have been thrilled, but now she scarcely even thought about it. In the middle of the first night at sea the weather had changed and it had turned grey and cold and rather rough. She was a good sailor and did not mind the waves, but the sharp drop in the temperature was an added trial. She had hoped for at least a few more days of sunbathing.

It was raining when they sailed up the river towards Vigo and everything was lost in mist. Mrs Chester said at breakfast:

"We shan't go ashore, and you can't go alone, Drina."

"Maybe I could go with the Barlows," said Drina. The Barlows were a pleasant, happy-go-lucky family with whom she had grown rather friendly.

"Well, that would be all right. I'll ask them."

The liner tied up close to the impressive Customs'
building and Drina went ashore with the Barlows. It
was exciting to walk through the Customs' Hall and out
through the gates into the unknown city, even though
the rain was still falling softly and everywhere looked
very grey. Vigo climbed the hills, most of the buildings
as grey as the sky, and there was certainly nothing that
corresponded with the usual pictures of sunny Spain.

They walked up a narrow cobbled street towards the
main shopping centre and Drina looked round her with
wide, noticing eyes. People did not seem to be wearing
colourful clothes, and it was odd to see young girls and
old women carrying baskets and milk-cans on their
heads. This ancient mode of carrying things gave them
a wonderfully erect appearance, but looked strange
when they were wearing ordinary modern clothes.

The Barlows only wanted to buy souvenirs, so Drina
said that she just wanted to climb to the Castello on the
hill. Mrs Barlow said:

"Very well, dear. You've got your map, though
personally I never can read one. We'll just be about here
somewhere. We'll probably have coffee later at that café
on the corner over there."

Drina climbed the steep streets until she reached the
foot of the hill and soon she was climbing much more
steeply, up narrow paths between grass. There were
wild flowers and she stopped to examine some of them,
pleased to find little blue scabious, one of the flowers of
her beloved chalk country. High on the hill she should
have had a superb view, but it was still misty and the
city was only dimly seen, with a suggestion of
encircling hills and water.

"The rain in Spain *doesn't* fall mainly in the plain,"
Drina thought, remembering Pygmalion, and, feeling
chilly, she hurried down the hill again.

Later she found the old part of the town and there she wandered very happily along the narrow cobbled lanes, where the old grey houses nearly met overhead. No one took any notice of her and she wondered if perhaps it was because she was so dark. There were advantages in not looking English.

In a cobbled square in the old part of the city was the twin-towered church of Santa Maria and Drina slipped inside, only to find that a Requiem Mass was just starting. Candles flared and the wonderful rise and fall of plain chant filled the big building. She stood quietly by the door, watching the faces of the people, especially the old women, and for a time – an unnoticed watcher at that Spanish funeral – her personal unhappiness faded and she was caught up in some of the old awareness.

"I am in Spain … in Spain."

An hour before they sailed again, a team of Galician dancers and their musicians came on board and gave a performance on the dance floor. Drina loved Spanish dancing but had never expected such a treat. The music grew wild and exciting and the dancers, some of them very young, moved with tremendous verve and speed. Drina stood with tightly clasped hands, her foot moving restlessly in time to the beat of the music.

Then it was over and the dancers, laughing, streamed away down the gangway just before it was removed. The rain still fell in a steady drizzle, but they did not seem to mind. They stood there on the quay, laughing and waving. Then, as the great ship moved slowly away, the musicians began to play again.

Drina gripped the wet rail and blinked back tears. All her life the sailing of a big ship was always to move her and there was something about being played away from Spain in the rain that was almost unbearably poignant.

A moment that she would never forget, to be treasured along with all her other special memories.

As they sailed away down the waterway, past the mist-shrouded islands, she continued to stand on deck. The holiday was almost over and soon they would be home again. Then her problems would really begin, for it could not be anything but painful to say goodbye to the Westminster flat, to her friends and the Dominick.

But she had made her decision and she could not show less courage than Jenny. She would have to put a brave face on it and go forward to deal with the new life.

DRINA

Follow Drina's fortunes, from her first ballet lessons to her triumphant appearances on stages throughout the world, in the popular Drina series of books.

Ballet for Drina	£2.99 ☐
Drina's Dancing Year	£2.99 ☐
Drina Dances in Exile	£2.99 ☐
Drina Dances in Italy	£2.99 ☐
Drina Dances Again	£2.99 ☐
Drina Dances in New York	£2.99 ☐
Drina Dances in Paris	£2.99 ☐
Drina Dances in Madeira	£2.99 ☐
Drina Dances in Switzerland	£2.99 ☐
Drina Goes on Tour	£2.99 ☐
Drina, Ballerina	£2.99 ☐

All Simon & Schuster Young Books are available at your local bookshop or can be ordered direct from the publisher. Just tick the titles you want and fill in the form below. Prices and availability subject to change without notice.

Simon & Schuster Cash Sales Department, PO Box 11, Falmouth, Cornwall, TR10 9EN, England.

Please enclose a cheque or postal order to the value of the cover price and allow the following for postage and packing:
UK: 80p for the first book, and 20p for each additional book ordered up to a maximum charge of 2.00.
BFPO: 80p for the first book, and 20p for each addition book.
OVERSEAS & EIRE: £1.50 for the first book, £1.00 for the second book, and 30p for each subsequent book.

Name ....

Address ....

....

Postcode ....